# OUT OF BREATH

# OUT OF BREATH

*A novel by Blair Richmond*

www.AshlandCreekPress.com

Out of Breath
*A novel by Blair Richmond*

Published by Ashland Creek Press
www.ashlandcreekpress.com

© 2011 Ashland Creek Press
All rights reserved
ISBN 978-0-9796475-7-4

Library of Congress Control Number: 2011930904

Printed in the United States of America on acid-free paper.
All paper products used to create this book are Sustainable Forestry Initiative (SFI) Certified Sourcing.

Cover and book design by John Yunker.

# OUT OF BREATH

*Our wills and fates do so contrary run.*

— William Shakespeare, *Hamlet*

# Part One:
# Lithia, Again

# One

They call it a runner's high, a sensation of euphoria experienced after a certain distance, usually a very long distance. Some runners must travel six miles or more before feeling it. But me, I feel that high every moment my worn old running shoes touch the ground.

Since I was eight years old I've been a runner. Not a jogger. A runner. I was always the fastest girl I knew and, during junior high, faster than any boy I knew. I ran cross-country at West Houston High, and I won state during my junior year. A scholarship to a major college seemed all but inevitable until my dad backed the car over my left foot the summer before my senior year. It's funny how quickly dreams can be crushed. Just as easily as my left foot.

The community college didn't have a running team, not that it mattered. I was too busy waiting tables and tending bar to have the time anyway. My foot eventually grew strong again, and I ran on my own when I found the time, usually late at night. Running was the only thing that kept me sane and out of trouble. I wish I had been running during that last night in Houston.

But because I wasn't, I guess that's why I'm running now. Though not in the conventional form. I've been *on* the run, moving from town to town, scrubbing floors at truck stop restrooms to pay for meals, sleeping in homeless shelters, keeping an eye open at all times. Never fully sleeping. Never relaxed.

Being on the run is different from running. For one thing, on the run, there's no such thing as a runner's high.

———

It is late in October when I arrive in Lithia. A woman in a huge white pickup truck with a white dog named Kitty on her lap gave me a ride north from Redding. She told me about the jerk who left her last month for a younger woman. She told me you can't pump your own gas in Oregon, not that I'll have to bother either way. She told me that people get lost in these parts; they pull over one day to check out the scenery and they never come back. She shoves ten dollars in my hand as I climb down from the cab.

"Be careful, kiddo," she says. "This town is full of crazies."

I watch her pull away and realize that I forgot to thank her. Her gift is the only money I have. Ten bucks won't buy me a motel room, so I begin looking for a place to sleep for the night.

I try to remember Lithia, searching the recesses of a child's memory. The town is in southern Oregon, so small and so close to the state line that if you're driving south on the interstate, you can miss it entirely and not realize it until you're in California. A speck of a city clinging to the forested legs of a sprawling wilderness of trees. People call Lithia "quaint." They come from all around to see shows at its theaters. But I have a different reason for coming here.

I was only eight when I left Lithia, and maybe that's why I have no memories of the town, or maybe it is just too dark tonight. There is no moon above, or if there is, it's denied viewing by the low-hanging clouds. I can see the beginning of the hills behind the small town square. Houses rising up, growing more expansive as the hills stretch into the white mist.

But the town square is well lit and lively with couples and young people milling about. Families, their little kids leashed to their hands; some older couples, retired and practically living at the theater. People my age, dressed in fatigues or batiks, hair knotted and dreadlocked, beards down to their chests, rings through their ears down to their shoulders. Music drifts down from the second floor of an old brick building. I sit on a bench and let the music calm me.

People look at me as they pass. I don't look like anyone here. I'm not quite a hippie, not a young mom, not a college student. I'm not one of the runners who comes here for training in the mountains; I'm not a theater buff. I don't fit in, even though I'm probably one of the few people who was actually born here.

There's a pizza shop on the edge of the square, and I spend half my money on a slice and a large coffee. I don't normally eat pizza but right now I'm so hungry I could order an entire pie. Yet I resist. I have to make the money last. Hunger is a fact of life now, and there's nothing to do but ignore it.

Same with the cold. When I left Houston, I didn't have time to pack much. Working my way through community college, I didn't own much anyway. And back then, there was no need for a jacket, not in the heat of the summer.

I headed for Austin, where I lied my way into a bartending job, adding two years to my life and saying I was twenty-one. Drunk men staring at me in my requisite low-cut tank top and jean shorts was a small price to pay for tips. It was the tips that had kept me in school back in Houston, and I got over the indignity of flaunting what I had for strangers a long time ago. Not that I have much to flaunt, with a runner's build, but I do have good legs.

Austin was a paradise. The bar owner was a salty woman who had inherited the bar from her ex-husband after he died—"He forgot to change the will, bless his dumb old heart," she said—and every night after closing she walked me back to my motel room, waiting till I was locked in safe before going home herself. I risked working there for a few weeks to save up money, but in the end it was still too close to Houston, so I moved on. I found a homeless shelter in Lubbock. Then one morning, after I woke up on my cot with a smelly man rolling back and forth on top of me, I left the state of Texas for good.

I headed north and then drifted west. As summer slipped into fall, I picked up a sweatshirt in Colorado Springs, a hoodie in Reno.

I didn't realize it at first, but from the very beginning, I was headed home. To Lithia.

So here I am, and though I'm wearing every piece of clothing I own right now, still I'm frozen through. I move to a spot that's close to a flamethrower—a woman with a baton burning at both ends. She's wearing a long, gauzy skirt, and I worry about it catching fire until I see a fire extinguisher next to her tip jar. I look at it with longing, all those bills and coins, but there's a guy sitting really close, and I'm not sure I could steal from her anyway.

The flames don't offer enough heat to keep me warm, so I stand and start walking again. I enter a park just off the town square and walk past a duck pond. I hear a creek running. A couple, hand in hand, pass me, and then I'm alone in the darkness, invisible. But I welcome it. I'm tired of the eyes that seem to judge me, take pity on me. Or worse. This is why I used to run at night, in spite of the warnings against it. Nobody could catch me anyway, I always believed. And I was right—nobody ever did.

I find a bench and consider making this my bed for the night. There's a public bathroom just beyond. Maybe I can withstand the cold. Maybe. Then I notice the sign on the bathroom building.

WARNING
RECENT BEAR ATTACKS
PROCEED WITH CAUTION
AVOID PARK AFTER DARK

My stomach clenches, triggered by a childhood memory I'm not expecting yet always dreading. I quickly turn around and escape the darkness of the park.

I return to the pizza shop and spend the rest of my money on pizza so that I can sit in the warmth, with all the good smells of pizza bread and the familiar smell of spilled beer. I take a table next to the window so I can watch people pass.

I'll have to leave eventually—then what? Even if I find a homeless shelter, I don't want to spend the night there. I'm tired of shelters and their rules and the men who inevitably sneak into the women's dorms. I don't like bunk beds, and I get claustrophobic when I'm lying in a room full of cots, listening to everybody breathe around me. Lately I've been looking for hiding places to sleep, places tucked away and warm, where nobody can find me or bother me. Where I can be alone.

The pizza shop closes, and I'm back on the street, now much emptier, quieter. I keep walking and find myself in a crowd of people, hundreds of them streaming from wide-open doors.

It's a theater, and I bask in the warmth of the crowds, probably the only person here who doesn't mind getting shoved around, bumped into.

I push against the current and into the theater. People everywhere, coming and going and talking and cleaning up. I work my way down a flight of stairs, then another, seeking out the quieter areas. One door leads to a dark room, a closet. I wait. It's warm here, and I sit on my fingers to warm them up. Soon I'm able to move my toes again.

An hour passes, or maybe more. When I finally open the door again, all is quiet, and I venture out. I wander through the dark hallways, guiding myself along by feeling the walls stretch out in front of me, until they curve around and up and I find myself in the theater, tripping over a row of seats and looking down on the stage, barely lit by little floor lights.

The stage is made to look like a bedroom, and I walk down the steps, pausing every so often to make sure I'm still alone. I step up onto the stage and stand above the bed. It's real—it has a soft mattress and a bedspread, even if there aren't any sheets underneath. I look around. Still alone. There's a fake window that's darkened out, a nightstand, a mirror. When I look into it, I see a pale face, a ghost of a girl. Her hair is in a mussed-up blonde ponytail and she looks hunched over and worn out and grubby.

But she is smiling, even if it looks as though she's forgotten how. She knows she's about to get the first good night's sleep she's had in months.

# Two

"Hey. You. Wake up!"

I open my eyes and, squinting in the bright light, see a man standing above me, his face red with anger. I blink and realize I am in bed, on a stage. The lights in the theater are on. And there is a man in a janitor's uniform yelling at me.

"Who are you?" he demands.

"I'm sorry." I scramble out of bed as fast as I can, grabbing my shoes and backpack off the floor in one quick motion. Then I hop off the stage and start up the aisle. I can hear him shouting after me.

"Stop her!"

I pick up speed until I'm running. I follow the EXIT signs and make my way outside, and I keep running until I'm back in the square. I don't know what time it is, but I can tell it's early because most of the shops are still closed, even the pizza place.

My stomach reminds me that I'm hungry. But I have no money left. When I walk past the park, I see a homeless person holding a cardboard sign. I don't want to infringe on his territory, so I leave the square and head up Main Street.

As a rule, I try to avoid begging, but I can't claim never to have done it. I've always worked and saved and gotten by on as little as I could, but there were a few times when I had no choice. Like that afternoon in Colorado, when I stood outside a supermarket with a sign, a lot like the one the guy in the park has, handwritten and crumpled and asking for something, anything. Sometimes people look at you as if you need to get off your lazy butt and get a job already. They don't understand that it's not laziness that brought you there. Sometimes people are kind. In Boulder, they were very kind, and I ate that night.

Today, I'm as desperate as I was back in Boulder, but I'm determined not to beg. I continue up Main Street and watch the stores begin coming to life. Merchants start to set up tables out front, prop open doors, and put out water dishes for passing dogs. Despite their busyness, everyone smiles at me or says hello. I'm reminded of what a nice town it is—maybe I'm also remembering that my life back then was nice, too—and I don't want to leave. But I don't know how in the world I can stay.

I find a wooden bench and sit, watching people. A block

away, a man has begun strumming an acoustic guitar, and I feel like closing my eyes. I always hear better with my eyes closed. With the music and the sun shining on my face, I feel lucky to be here, to be free. I try to force thoughts of the future from my mind. Right here, right now, I am content. And that counts for something.

I spend the morning wandering from bench to bench, seeking sun and music, both easy to find on one of the fall's last warm days. For a while I sit near a woman playing the flute and watch her with interest. She can't be much older than I am, and she's wearing a crown of flowers in her hair and a green dress that's all raggedy at the bottom, as if she lives in a forest. Her music lulls me into something like peace.

Finally my growling stomach wins out, and I feel light-headed as I begin to walk again, wondering what I can do for money, for food. I have no instrument, no talents other than running. And right now I'm too weak even for that.

I ask a stranger for the time, if for no other reason than to interact with someone. He is friendly and tells me it is two o'clock, much later than I thought. I need to eat.

I turn off Main Street and make my way away from the high hills behind me to the flatter part of town. The houses here are smaller than the ones along the hill, and older, even though some of them have been renovated to look brand-new. The street comes to an end at a set of railroad tracks. Two empty railroad cars wait idly on the tracks, as if they might run again someday.

I follow the tracks to a small shopping plaza, jammed with cars and people. A sign reads LITHIA FOOD CO-OP, and another beggar stands near the parking lot entrance. I walk into the store. I don't know why, since I have no money, but maybe they'll have some samples.

Inside, everything smells fresh, from the vegetables stacked high in wooden crates to the simmering foods in the take-out area. I wander through the produce section, plucking a few organic grapes when no one is looking. Past the cheese shop are the bulk-food bins—rice and beans and lentils and other things I can't nibble on, but also nuts and dates and candied ginger. I slip my hands into the bins as often as I dare, but none of it is enough. It seems as though these little bites of food are only waking up my hunger, and I can hear my stomach literally groaning.

I pick up a bottle of orange juice and walk around the store, wondering if I can drink it and deposit the bottle someplace without being seen. Employees are rushing around, busy. But I'm not a thief. I put the juice back.

As I do, I glimpse a tofu sandwich, wrapped in plastic and ready to eat. It was made yesterday and is on sale, half off, only three dollars, which of course I don't have. I pace back and forth in front of the prepared-foods refrigerator. I hate myself right now, for what I'm about to do. But I do it anyway.

I pass the fridge one last time, reaching over and sliding the sandwich into the left pocket of my hoodie. I step toward the door as slowly and nonchalantly as I can, blood rushing to my head because I feel as though everyone is staring at me. I try to walk out but realize that I'm trying to exit through an entrance-only door, so I have to turn back. More self-conscious than ever, I pretend to shop some more. It gives me a chance to make sure nobody's following me. When I glance over my shoulder, I see only a woman with a toddler behind me.

I'm pretending to peruse the selection of pineapples when I get an opportunity. The toddler begins to cry as his mother leads him out through the automatic doors. Then he starts to scream, digging in his heels and refusing to take another step. I thank the universe for unruly children as I start past them. A screaming child always commands more attention than a small young woman slipping out the door. Even if her pocket is bulging with stolen food.

Outside, I breathe a sigh of relief. I'm about to turn the corner and quicken my pace when I feel a strong hand on my arm.

"Hold it right there."

I turn to face one of the co-op clerks. He's young, like me, and his thin, goateed face has a serious look on it.

"What is it?" I ask, trying to look innocent.

"You have something that belongs to the store. Something you did not pay for."

I look around for the fastest escape route. It's a habit I've been able to perfect over the years, finding the quickest way out of a bar, or a motel, or a shelter dormitory. I feel my legs tensing, ready to propel me like a deer from this parking lot and through the alley, to take me out of this town for good, once and for all.

"I think you're mistaken," I say.

"Then what's that in your pocket? And don't say you're just happy to see me." He is smiling now, the serious look gone. Even though his joke is really lame, I feel my body relaxing. Is he going to let me off the hook?

"Please don't call the cops," I say, still uncertain. "I'm out of money and I'm really hungry. I'll return it. I haven't even touched it, see?" I reach inside my pocket and remove the sandwich.

"Tofu sandwiches pair well with our organic orange juice," he says. "I see that you and I have a similar palate."

So he saw me with the juice, too. "I didn't take that juice." I hold up my arms, as if inviting him to search my pockets. "I promise."

But he doesn't frisk me; instead, he hands me the juice container that he saw me contemplating in the store. He must've been following me all along. I'm embarrassed that he witnessed me drooling over all that food, and still a little worried that maybe he's already called the cops.

I shove the juice back and give him the sandwich at the same time. "Look, I don't know what you're up to, but I haven't eaten anything so please just take it back and I'll go, okay?"

"Don't worry," he says. He takes my hand and pulls out my clenched fist, revealing my palm. He places the sandwich there and puts the juice in my other hand. "I paid for this, as well as your sandwich. Enjoy it."

I stare at the food in my hand. "I don't get it."

"I get an employee discount." He smiles again, then shrugs. "You looked like you could use a break. But don't do it again, okay? I don't want to lose my job. There's a food bank about six blocks from here. They've probably even got tofu."

A vegetarian-friendly food bank—only in Lithia. Certainly not in Texas. I want to throw my arms around him, I'm so happy, but instead I nod until my head feels as though it'll bobble off my neck. "Thanks. Thanks a lot."

I watch him return to the store. Perhaps this was a sign, the sign I needed. Maybe Lithia is a place I can still call home after all.

I go to the park to eat. I sit near the pond and pull apart the sandwich with my fingers, making every bite last as long as I can. A couple of ducks glide past me on the water, mumbling to themselves, and they stop in front of me, hanging out at the water's edge, begging for a piece of bread. I know I shouldn't feed them, me of all people, but I toss down a small piece. From one beggar to another.

The day is aging quickly, but it's still nice and warm. The deciduous trees are losing their green, and even the pine needles are dry and dying. I walk back through town, suddenly wanting to be among people, though I don't know why because it's not something I normally enjoy. But Lithia feels better to me somehow. It's amazing how one act of kindness can make an entire town, even an entire world, seem friendly.

The courtyard around the theater complex is crowded. I see that there was a matinee on the Elizabethan stage. *Hamlet.* I've never seen *Hamlet,* have never even read any Shakespeare. Shakespeare wasn't among the courses offered at the community college I went to.

I keep walking, past the restaurants and shops. Then I see the shoes. A bright new pair of Brooks running shoes whose blue-and-yellow coloring seems to mirror the sky. I can't help but look down at the shoes on my feet. They're the same brand—if there's one investment worth making, it's in good shoes—but they're more than four years old and worn past the point of recognition. The rubber bottom has completely worn off my left shoe, and the right has a gaping hole tearing through the toe.

As if possessed by a force I can't control, I go inside and

find the shoe on the wall. I take it from its little metal shelf and hold it up, breathing in its new-shoe smell. The untested nylon. The freshly stamped and glued rubber soles. It's as yummy to me as a bakery is to a normal person.

"You want to try on a pair?"

I turn to see a tall blonde woman watching me. She's wearing a T-shirt that reads LITHIA RUNNERS.

"Oh." I put the shoe back. "No, thanks. I'm just looking."

She stares down at my feet, dubious. "Looks like you could use a new pair."

"I can't afford them."

"Well, why don't you try them on, just to get a feel for them. Let me guess, eight and a half?"

"Yeah, but—"

"I'll be right back."

The woman exits into a back room, and I sigh. Trying on new running shoes will be like being in that co-op—the temptation will be too great. A sandwich is one thing, but a hundred-dollar pair of running shoes is another. And after this morning, I'm not sure what I'm capable of anymore.

I have to get out of here. I'm on my way out when a flyer on the bulletin board near the door catches my eye. It's advertising an upcoming race called "Cloudline." A half marathon, only a few weeks away. I feel my legs growing twitchy, eager to be running again.

"Have you run Cloudline?"

It's that woman—she's back again, standing over my shoulder, a shoebox in her hand.

"No."

"It's brutal. It climbs up the side of Mount Lithia—one vertical mile."

"Sounds like fun."

She laughs. "We runners are such masochists, aren't we? Good thing I chose to marry another one—the only person who ever really gets it is another runner. I'm Stacey, by the way. My fiancé and I own this place."

I pause before telling her, "I'm Kat."

"Well, Kat, let's get these shoes on you," Stacey says, holding up the box.

"That's okay," I say. "I really should be going."

"Are you sure?" She looks down at my feet again. "Really, Kat, you shouldn't be walking around in those things. Bad shoes can affect your knees, your back, cause all sorts of problems. If you really are a runner, you have to take better care of your feet."

"If you think my shoes are scary, you don't want to see my socks."

"Is that it? I can get you new ones. We keep a few pairs on hand for people who walk in with sandals and that sort of thing."

Stacey crosses the room in three steps, and the next thing I know a pair of white athletic socks is hurtling toward me. "Think fast!" she calls out, and I grab the socks just before they hit me in the head. They are so white and clean I want to press them against my cheek.

I slowly untie the laces of my decrepit shoes, and I'm grateful when another customer walks in and Stacey turns away. Hurriedly I take off my shoes, revealing socks that are stained so dark with dirt and sweat it's hard to believe they were ever white. Both of my big toes burst out of the fabric as if they're trying to make a prison break. I quickly remove the socks and slip on the new ones. They are so soft I never want to take them off. I stuff my old socks into my pocket.

Then, the shoes. After I put them on, I stand and feel half an inch taller, my old shoes so flattened by mileage and weather and time that it was like I'd shrunk. I'm five foot three and a half, but in these shoes I can claim five-four without getting doubtful looks.

"They fit you well," says Stacey, walking back toward me. I see that someone else is helping the other customer now, a man at the cash register wearing the same LITHIA RUNNERS T-shirt. There's a small pile of clothing on the counter, running pants and shirts, a hat. What a luxury, I think, to be able to walk into a store like this and buy anything you want.

"What do you say?" Stacey continues. "Should I hold

them for you until you have the money?"

"That might be a very long hold," I say. "I sort of have to find a job first."

She turns away. "Honey, come over here," she calls to the man in the other LITHIA RUNNERS shirt. "That's my fiancé, David," she tells me as he hands the customer a receipt. When he comes over, I notice that they're about the same height, both a head taller than I am, both muscular and strong, though David is longer and leaner.

"David, this is Kat—" Stacey looks at me, waiting for my last name. I don't have time to think, so I give her the first name that pops into my head.

"Jones."

"This is Kat Jones. She's new in town."

"Oh, welcome. I see you're getting off on the right foot." He laughs, but Stacey and I only stare at him. "Come on," he says. "That's at least sort of funny, isn't it?"

"Not really, honey. Listen, do we need any part-time help?"

"Not unless you start slacking off."

"Don't tempt me," Stacey says.

David tilts his head toward the storeroom. "Hang on, I think I hear the fax machine. Be right back."

"Coward," Stacey says, rolling her eyes. "Give me a sec."

She follows him to the back, and I return to the Cloudline

flyer and study the details. I grew up in the imposing shadow of Mount Lithia, gazing up at it from town, from the shorter hills I used to climb as a kid. This run looks brutal. A vertical climb of 5,300 feet. Fog and snow likely along the route. I want to run it, badly. I want to conquer this mountain. To prove that life hasn't conquered me.

Stacey returns with David wrapped around one arm, both of them smiling.

"Kat, how would you like a little part-time work?" David asks.

"I—well, I wouldn't want to impose," I say, looking from one of them to the other. I have the same feeling I had at the co-op, that this must be some sort of joke, that it's impossible for people to be this kind.

"You're not imposing," Stacey says. "With Cloudline coming up, we get a surge of runners from around the region. They need shoes. They need gloves. They need jackets. It's our version of the Boston Marathon."

"It's not permanent or anything," David says. "Just a few weeks."

"That's great. That's perfect. I'll do whatever you need."

"You can start tomorrow at ten," says Stacey. "You'll help me open the store."

"Okay."

"What's your phone number?" Stacey asks, picking up a

pen from the counter.

"Um. I don't have one."

"Address?"

"Not yet."

"You mean you don't have a place to live?"

"I'm still looking," I say. "I just got into town yesterday. But I can be here at ten, no problem."

She and David exchange a look. "We've got a small studio out back, behind our house," Stacey says. "It used to be a garage but we got it all fixed up, with a little kitchenette and a bathroom and everything. You can stay there tonight. And tomorrow we'll work out a rental agreement."

"Really?"

I see Stacey's grip tighten around David's arm. "David, you do not hear that fax machine again," she says, then adds, to me, "Yes, I'm sure. It's not the Ritz, but you can afford it."

"How do you know?"

She grins. "Because I know what you're making."

She digs around in a drawer and finds her purse, pulling a single key off her keychain. "Come on," she says, "let's go take a look. We're only a few blocks away."

She leads me out the back door, through an alley, down sidewalks covered with dead leaves. They crunch under our feet.

"Why are you being so nice to me?" I ask.

"I don't know," she says. "It must be the water."

"The water?"

"Lithia Springs," she says. "You never heard about the springs?"

I have only a vague memory of the water, so I shake my head.

"Our water comes from natural springs that contain traces of lithium. Lithium has been used for years to improve moods. That's what put this town on the map a hundred years ago. People from around the country would travel here to drink the water, soak in it. They thought it had healing properties, too."

"Does it?"

"Beats me." We turn down a quiet street, the trees forming a canopy above us. "I don't drink it," she adds. "Stinks too much."

"What does it smell like?" I ask.

Stacey smiles at me as she leads me down a brick walkway and opens the door to the cottage. "Remind me to show you the fountain in the town square. You can't live in Lithia without drinking from the springs."

As she says that, a memory resurfaces—of someone holding me up to the fountain in the square, of a sulfur-like smell, of me spitting water out, of laughter.

"We have a filter on the faucet in here," Stacey says, "so

you won't notice the smell."

The cottage is beautiful. It's tiny, with only two windows, but its old wood floors are whitewashed, and it's painted in light blue and white, like a cloud-dusted sky. I peek into the bathroom, which is sparkling clean, the nicest bathroom I've seen in ages.

"I'll bring you some towels," Stacey says, "and you'll join us for dinner. Most of the time, we just grab take-out because we're working right through. But the co-op has good healthy stuff. Do you know the co-op?

"Um." I feel my ears burn and imagine they must be bright red. "I think I saw a sign, yeah."

"I'll have David pick up some bread and juice for you while he's there. Just so you'll have a little something in the morning. Busy day tomorrow."

I look around the little room—a place of my own, after all these months. For now, anyway. Then I look at Stacey, at her kind face. She is so tall I have to stretch my neck backward. "How can I ever thank you?"

"Tell you what," she says. "You can accept those Brooks as an advance on your salary and go for a run with me tomorrow. I'm behind in my Cloudline training and need a running buddy who won't smoke me the way David does."

"You're on."

# Three

This morning, a couple walks up to me and asks where the theater is. And I tell them—just like that, with confidence, like I've lived here all my life. It's been a week, and I'm starting to wish I *can* live here for the rest of my life. I have a place to sleep. I have a job. And I love being around shoes and people who love the outdoors as much as I do.

And then there is running. Every morning before work, I go out for a quick run, each time in a different direction, with no idea how far I will go or what I will see. Yesterday, I went north, wandering through the residential streets until I nearly ran right into a family of deer. I startled them—a mother and father and two younger ones—and they all jerked their heads up and stood frozen, staring at me with their big eyes wide and their ears focused on me like satellite dishes. I stopped and waited as they tiptoed across the street. I've seen them eating the vegetation outside my cottage, wandering through back-yards and open grassy lots. The deer are year-round residents of Lithia, Stacey told me, and she likes them, too—*They do my weeding for me*, she said—but she also said that not all the homeowners share our enthusiasm. I don't see why not; the deer are so peaceful. I love their silence most of all.

My first customer of the day is an elderly woman who is trying on her first pair of running shoes. She just retired here from Los Angeles, and she wants to start working out.

"Better late than never," she says.

"Running will change your life," I tell her. "It changed mine."

After work, Stacey invites me for a run up the hill. Even though I ran this morning, I'm excited to go out again. She changes her clothes in the back. Me, I'm already ready to go; I don't have much else to wear other than running shorts and T-shirts, and I've been wearing my new shoes everywhere.

While Stacey is still in back, David approaches, his voice low. "Is she taking you up the Lost Mine Trail?"

"I think so," I say. "We went up there yesterday, but we didn't make it all that far. It's quite a climb."

He looks worried. "Stay together," he says.

"What do you mean?"

"Keep an eye on each other," he says. "Don't let her out of your sight."

"Bears?" I ask. His anxiety is a little catching.

"Stacey says I'm paranoid, but there have been attacks up there. Just last month, a tourist in town for the theater went missing."

"Don't worry. I'll look out for her."

He smiles. "By the way, you're doing great. I wish I could hire you permanently."

"That's okay. I'll find something."

———

Tonight, Stacey leads me through town to the Lost Mine Trail. Just getting to the trailhead is no simple feat. We start up Frontier Street, which climbs sharply for several hundred feet. Then we turn right onto Highview Drive and follow it along two arching switchbacks, passing ever-grander mansions that cling to the side of the hill.

As we heave our way up, she tells me about Lithia's theaters, how these three stages have supported the town for decades, bringing in tourists from around the world. "When I first came here five years ago," she says, huffing a little, "it was to be an actress. I didn't get offered a role that first season, so I worked for an accountant. And then there was David."

"How'd you meet?"

"Met him at the store, first day he opened. He'd just

retired—he sold his software company when he was thirty and moved up here, bought the store to keep himself busy. I'd just started running myself, so I went in and found the whole place a mess. Poor guy's great at software but doesn't know the first thing about inventory or customer relations. So I became employee number one."

Eventually the paved road turns to gravel, then dirt, then narrows to a trail. I glance over my shoulder to take one last look at the town below. We must've gained at least five hundred feet in elevation—Lithia looks so small from up here. Then we enter the forest.

The Lost Mine Trail is a winding trail that meanders up the side of the Siskiyou National Forest and continues for hundreds of miles. It connects with the Pacific Crest Trail, that two-thousand-mile trail that committed (or crazy) hikers can take from San Diego all the way up to Canada. But even this part of the Lost Mine Trail is also for committed (or crazy) runners, and it's pretty desolate; we've seen no one else since leaving town. *I promised David that I wouldn't run on this trail alone in the evening*, Stacey said when she first brought me up here, but when she rolled her eyes, I knew she did anyway.

Stacey is a strong runner, with a longer stride than I have, but I keep pace with her. I can hear her breathing grow louder, and soon we cease our conversation. She stops talking first, and I wonder if she's been pushing herself because I'm here, or if she's testing me.

I'm tempted to pull ahead of her, to prove that I can do more than just keep pace, but I'm too grateful to her to risk showing her up. Runners are a strange lot. I've seen friendships formed and lost based on who is faster, and most of us can't help being competitive. I wouldn't want anything to come between our new friendship.

The sun has fallen behind Mount Lithia, and the forest grows more dense until the darkness forces me to blink my eyes to adjust.

I remember what David said, and I stick close to Stacey, though I feel her trying to pull ahead. Now it's me who's pushing too hard; I feel my lungs straining for oxygen, and I'm trying hard to breathe through a cramp in my side.

Suddenly, I hear a noise in the brush on my right.

I stop and try to listen, but I can only hear my breath. Stacey stops a few yards ahead.

"What's wrong?"

"I heard something."

"Probably just a bear."

I look at her and she's smiling. "More likely a deer," she assures me.

"That's not funny," I say. "David said we should be careful up here." I peer into the thick grove of trees, hoping to see a pair of big deer eyes, a pair of wide ears. I can't see anything, but I feel as though something is staring back at me, and my skin tingles with fear.

Stacey walks down the hill to me and looks into the forest. "David likes to worry about me," she says. "I did see a bear once, a year ago. I think I scared him more than he scared me."

"What about the missing tourist?"

"I don't know. Lithia attracts all types of people, and lots of them come and go. Some people even live up here."

"Really?"

"Hill people. Tree-huggers. True survivalists. They come out of the hills for food and supplies, or just supplies. Then they come back up here."

I still have that uneasy feeling, like we're being watched, but I don't tell Stacey.

"Maybe we should head back," I say, trying to make my voice sound casual. "Let the deer get back to her dinner."

I don't know who it is I'm trying to reassure.

# Four

David and Stacey live in a two-story, gray-and-white Victorian on Fifth Street, in a section known as the Pioneer District. While the streets up on the side of the hill have fancy names, the streets down here are numbered and form a grid.

It's the oldest part of town, running along the railroad tracks that used to connect Lithia with cities north and south. The trains no longer run here, but the tracks remain, as if hopeful that they will again.

David insists on calling my new digs The Guest House, but I think of it as The Cottage: it's cozy, with its one room, small bathroom, and shower. It's furnished with a double bed, a desk, a chair, and a bookcase. There are storage bins under the bed, which is where I'd put my clothes if I had any. There's not much room—it wouldn't fit more than two people—but

I'm used to small spaces and I feel right at home. Best of all, it's quiet and all mine.

The studio has a skylight; in the morning, the sun gleams straight into my eyes and wakes me up. I grab an apple from the tiny fridge below the desk. There are some used paperbacks in the bookcase, and I pick up one as I eat my breakfast. I have an hour before work.

I hear footsteps outside the door, then a knock. "You decent?"

It's Stacey. I open the door.

"I've got extra eggs if you want some," she says. She's holding a plate piled high with scrambled eggs and toast.

"Thanks," I say, "but I try not to eat eggs."

"Oh?" She seems disappointed. "Allergic?"

"No, I'm a vegan."

"Ah," she says. "Well, David will be happy to hear that."

"Why?"

"He's vegan, too. He'll be glad to have you around. Until now, he's been stuck with me, the recovering vegan."

I give Stacey a quizzical look.

"I try," she explains, "but sometimes I fall off the wagon. Like these eggs here. And maybe the occasional burger. David doesn't need to hear that, though."

"My lips are sealed."

"What are you doing after work tonight?"

"Let me check my schedule," I joke.

"Have you ever seen *Hamlet*?"

"No."

"We've got an extra ticket with your name on it, if you're up for a little culture."

———

As I walk through Lithia Theater Plaza with Stacey and David, I feel as though I'm on a stage myself. That is, I feel as though I'm in costume, playing a role.

Earlier, Stacey had taken me to the consignment shop next door to the running store, and she helped me pick out a dress. *An advance on your next paycheck*, she said, though she said that before and she still paid me the full amount, even when I protested.

Then, about twenty minutes before leaving for the theater, Stacey called me into the house and sat me down at the vanity in her bathroom. She studied my face, then made me close my eyes, and I felt brushes on my eyelids, cheeks, and nose. She turned me away from the mirror and told me to look at the ceiling, and I felt the tug of mascara on my eyelashes. She fussed with my hair a bit, then turned me back around.

I almost didn't recognize myself. My hair looked full and shiny, practically the only time I haven't worn it in a ponytail since arriving in Lithia. And my face looked so polished, almost sophisticated. I was so used to seeing myself either sweaty or dirty, I could hardly believe it was possible to look this nice. Before we went downstairs, Stacey had me try on a couple pairs of her shoes, but they were way too big. But she did loan me a pair of black onyx earrings that dangled low and swayed when I walked.

And now we're at the theater, crossing through the cobblestoned courtyard, becoming part of a slow crowd shuffling inside. My dress is beautiful—a dark midnight blue, made of a soft organic cotton, and long, going all the way down to my shoes and nearly covering them, which is good because all I have to wear are my new Brooks. But I still feel glamorous.

We find our seats, which are in the fifth row, right in the middle, and after a few moments the theater goes dark.

That's when I see him, seated on the stage. He'd been there all along, but I was too busy looking around to notice that he wasn't one of the stagehands. He's dressed in a fitted black suit—a gorgeous man, with dark hair and a slender build, and tall, even from where I sit, looking down on him.

Hamlet.

Actually, the actor who plays Hamlet. And I'm glad he's in the leading role because I don't want to take my eyes off him.

He carries himself with such confidence. I know he's an

actor playing a role, but I'm more focused on the actor than the role. Who is he? Does he live in Lithia? Is he single?

"To be or not to be," he says to himself, yet he's looking at me. Directly at me. I stare back and I feel my body burn, my face flush. He continues his soliloquy.

> To die, to sleep—
> To sleep—perchance to dream: ay, there's the rub,
> For in that sleep of death what dreams may come
> When we have shuffled off this mortal coil...

He looks away, and I hear myself exhale. I could've sworn he was looking at me. And he paused as he spoke—or was that part of the role? It's absurd even to think that he'd paused as he looked at me—he's a professional, after all—but a girl can dream, can't she?

I feel Stacey shift in her seat to my left, and I realize that she could have been the object of the actor's attention. I glance over at her. She, too, is focused on Hamlet. We all are. It was my imagination after all.

But as I watch him, this poor lonely character, I feel a bond. I want to reach out and help him, to ease his pain. And as the play ends, as we all stand up and applaud until our hands are numb, again I have to remind myself that this was a performance, that it wasn't real.

———w———

"That was amazing," I say, as we exit the theater into the frigid night. I can feel myself shivering even in the coat I borrowed from Stacey, but I don't care about the cold. I'm still sitting in the fifth row, staring down at Hamlet. Or whoever it was. "Thank you for taking me."

"Our pleasure," David says.

"The evening's not over just yet, you know," Stacey says. "We've got a party to attend."

"Really?"

"It's an annual thing," David says. "Since we support the theater with big bucks, each year we get invited to the cast party they throw toward the end of every season. A chance to mingle with the actors and directors."

"And drink outstanding wine," Stacey adds.

I follow them across the street and into an old brick building. "This was the old elementary school," David says. "The theater now uses it for meetings and events."

We enter a large room, decorated so beautifully that it takes me a few minutes to realize that it's the old gym, with high-arched windows and a child-sized stage at the far end. There are tables covered with black cloths, candles glittering on top of them, flowers everywhere, a huge buffet of food, a bar. People are milling around in much nicer clothes than I'm wearing, and definitely better shoes.

I follow Stacey to the bar, trying to keep my Brooks covered as much as I can. "Chardonnay, please," she tells the guy behind the bar, and then looks at me.

"Water's fine," I say. I think Stacey thinks I'm older than I am, and I don't want to correct her. Not yet, at least. I can't let anything jeopardize this: having a home, a good job, wonderful people to look after me. For so much of my life, little has gone the way I hoped. It's a life no one would want. A mother dead before I got to know her. A father grown mean by loss and failed jobs and alcohol. A budding college career cut short by circumstances that still give me nightmares and probably always will. But I feel like this is my big break, my chance to be happy. At last.

"There's the director," Stacey says, pointing to a short, plump man with long curly hair, dressed in jeans and a green sweater. "His name is Gerry Ross. He's a genius. Could direct anywhere in the world he wants, but for some reason he chooses to stay here in our little town."

I want to say that I know why he stays, but the room has grown so loud with voices and laughter that I doubt I'll be heard. "Come on, I'll introduce you," she says, but the thought of talking to strangers suddenly makes me nervous. So I ask her where the bathroom is, and I take my time getting back. By the time I return to the party, I can't see Stacey and David anywhere, so I stand in a corner, watching people, waiting for a glimpse of one of them.

Then I see him.

Hamlet.

He must have just arrived. People crowd around him, shaking his hand, slapping his back. Women hug him, and I find myself feeling jealous, wishing I were one of them. But though he is smiling cordially, I can tell there's no enthusiasm behind it. I'm surprised he can't hide it better. He must've used up all his acting energy for the play.

I watch him navigate through the crowd until he ends up off to one side of the room, until his back is against the wall and he is alone, just like me. I want to go say something to him, but I don't want to be like those other women. The women he tolerated and gave only fake smiles.

Maybe he'll notice me, like he did in the theater. But his eyes don't wander. They stare straight ahead, as if he's meditating or just bored. Maybe he's like me, a bit of a loner, awkward around people. Maybe he's trapped by his shyness, like I've been most of my life.

Before I realize it, I am walking toward him. I feel my heart quickening—I've never done anything like this before. I can handle myself well enough and can even be tough, but only if I have to be. I'm never bold, like this. Especially with guys like him. Guys who are so beautiful it's hard even to stand near them without blushing until you feel hotter than the sun.

And then I'm standing in front of him. "Hello," I say.

He's still gazing straight ahead, only he seems to be looking right through me instead of at me.

"I just wanted to tell you that I enjoyed your performance," I add.

Finally he raises his eyes. He looks at me with curiosity, but he doesn't say anything, and his silence makes me squirm. Bad idea. This was a very bad idea.

I've just turned to walk away when he speaks. "Have we met before?"

I turn back. "I don't think so."

"Are you quite sure?"

"Quite."

He studies me some more, as if he doesn't believe me. I take a step toward him, as if magnetically pulled in his direction. It's strange, and a little annoying. I've literally never been drawn to a guy this way before. But he seems to have some sort of inexplicable pull on me.

"I suppose you're right," he says. "I see so many faces. Too many. What's your name?"

"Kat."

"Is that short for Katherine?"

I nod.

"I'm Roman."

"It's nice to meet you. You were great tonight."

"You're a runner," he says, as if he hadn't heard me.

"How did you know?"

"You have a runner's build," he says, and I feel my face go warm as his eyes run down the length of my body, snug in my slim-fitting dress. But, I'm surprised to notice, he's not doing it in that leering way that I'm used to from the men I'd serve at dive bars. Instead, it's observant, almost clinical. He looks at me the way my childhood cat used to, with mild bemusement, as if he was the keeper of the world's secrets and I was a mere, lowly human.

"The shoes are another giveaway," he adds, and I look down to see the toes of my Brooks peeking out from under the skirt of the dress.

"I just moved here," I say. "Still unpacking."

"Welcome to Lithia, then. Perhaps sometime we can run together."

Before I can answer, I feel a hand on my shoulder, and I jump. "Fancy meeting you here," a voice says.

I turn to see the grocery clerk from the co-op. Instead of jeans and a T-shirt, he's wearing khakis and a button-down oxford. "I'm Alex."

"Oh, hi. I'm Kat."

"Kat who?"

"Just Kat." And then I turn back to Roman—but he's gone.

I glance all around but can't see him anywhere. How could he have disappeared so quickly?

"Did I interrupt?" Alex asks.

"Yes," I say, my eyes still searching the room. Then I come to my senses. "I mean, no. No." I force my attention back to Alex. "Hey, thanks again for the other day. I want to pay you back."

"Forget about it. I can't resist a vegan shoplifter."

I smile at him. "That sandwich was amazing."

"It looks like you've done well for yourself," he says, and he, too, is looking at my dress.

"I'm working at Lithia Runners. Part-time only, but it's a start."

"Congratulations. David and Stacey are awesome people."

"I know."

"Kat, would you be interested in going out sometime?"

This is a surprise, and I'm not sure what to say. "Um—"

"Anything you want. Dinner? Movie? Petty theft?"

"Very funny," I say.

The truth is, I'm stunned by the turn of events. In a matter of minutes, two handsome guys have made a pass at me. Maybe there really is something in the water.

Alex is cute, and I want to say yes, but already I can't get Roman out of my mind. And I probably shouldn't be bothering with men at all, given the way my luck has turned for the better. I want to keep it that way.

"I'm sorry, Alex. I—I'm just busy getting settled, finding a permanent job."

"I understand. No worries. Some other time maybe, when things settle down."

I watch Alex walk away into the crowd, and I wonder if I've made a mistake, saying no to a romantic night out in favor of the prospect of a trail run. But I'm a runner. Runners are strange people. Again, I scan the room for Roman, but he's definitely gone. As if he'd simply vanished.

# Five

A few days later, when I'm running with Stacey, I ask her about Roman. I wait until we are heading up toward the Lost Mine Trail, hoping she'll be too focused on the ascent to wonder why I'm so interested.

But she laughs, as if she's been expecting me to ask. "He's only the most eligible bachelor in Lithia," she says. "And this isn't a town crawling with bachelors, so you can imagine. He's also one of the youngest stars in the history of the Lithia Theater Company."

"How old is he?" It occurs to me just then that I hadn't been able to tell—there's something ageless about Roman's face.

"Not sure," she says. "Twenty-five, twenty-six? It's hard to tell."

"I can see why he's a star here. He's an amazing actor."

"Don't tell David," she says, "but I had a huge crush on Roman. Before David came to Lithia, of course."

"Really?"

"Oh, yeah. I mean, who doesn't? But it's a little embarrassing—I practically threw myself at him. He's the type of guy who won't even look at anyone at least five years younger, and here I am, five years older."

"He must have a lot of girlfriends."

"That's the weird thing," she says. "He's never had a girlfriend, at least not that I know of. He's not gay, as far as I can tell, because he's got plenty of guys who'd love to go out with him, too. He's just a loner, or a workaholic, or both." She gives me a sidelong look. "Are you hoping to be the one who gets him to change his mind?"

I feel my face turn redder than it already is from our uphill climb. "No, I'm just curious. I talked to him at the party last night."

"Just curious?" She laughs. "Yeah, so was I. So what'd you talk about?"

"He suggested we go for a run sometime."

Stacey goes silent. We've just entered the trail and are hitting steep dirt, and I can feel her beginning to pull away again. I don't have time to wonder why she keeps doing this; it takes too much energy to stay with her. I feel her glance over at me as we head deeper into the woods, and that's when I notice that it's beginning to get dark. The trail suddenly feels dangerous.

"You ready to turn around?" I ask, a prickle of some unknown fear running up my spine.

"Tired already?"

"I can hardly see the trail anymore."

"Wimp," she says. "You know, Roman is a night runner. If you want to be his new running buddy, you'd better get used to it."

A night runner—how does she know that?

Then she turns, so quickly that I trip as I try to follow her. I land on my left knee and feel a deep scratch, a twig or tree branch probably. She doesn't stop or even slow down. By the time I stand up, she's already around the bend. I guess I've struck a nerve.

I lean down to take a look at my bleeding knee—and then I hear it. A whisper. A man's voice.

That's enough to get me moving again, despite the painful scratch. I start down the hill, fast. But it's not fast enough. I hear that voice, whispering in words I don't understand. It's like another language, only it's not one I've ever heard before.

I stumble again and land face-first in the dirt. I hear a rustling noise—this time it's right in front of me—and I bite my lips to keep from screaming. I don't want to look up but I do.

It's a deer, standing on the trail right in front of me. Frozen. Frightened, like me.

I exhale, and with that the deer takes two quick steps and disappears back into the woods. I push myself to my feet and look behind me. The trail is empty.

I must have heard the wind. It was only the wind.

A hand grabs my shoulder. This time I do scream, whirling around and pulling myself away at the same time.

"Kat!" It's Stacey. "What's wrong with you?"

"Don't sneak up on me like that," I say.

"I looked back and you were gone." Then she looks at my knee. "Did you fall?"

I look down. Blood is dripping onto my new socks and shoes. I reach down and dab at the cut with my hands, but the sweat only mixes with the blood and stings. I'm worried about my new shoes. But then I hear another rustle in the woods, and I straighten up again. I look at Stacey and can tell that she heard it, too.

"Perhaps we should call it a day," she says, and I agree.

We head back to town at a slower pace, an easy jog, and she never acknowledges that she'd turned and left me behind. I'm starting to wonder if that was all in my imagination, and so I don't mention it either.

# Six

My two-week stint at Lithia Runners is nearing an end. To make it last a bit longer, I've asked for a day off to look for work. I spend the morning on a public computer at the Lithia Library. I find positions open at the city's parks department, a bakery, and a B&B. I'm excited by the prospects, but when I go to borrow a pen and some paper from the reference librarian, she warns me that getting a job in Lithia won't be easy. "It's a small town," she says, "and there are more people than jobs."

I decide to think positively, and I head for the bakery, which is only a five-minute walk from the library. The great thing about Lithia is that everything is within walking distance, which is lucky for me because I have a feeling I'll be forty before I own my own car.

At the bakery, I'm told I don't have enough experience. I

offer to work for free until I get the experience, but the owner, an older man who looks as though he's been up all night, doesn't bite. So I move on to the B&B, whose owner somehow thinks she can find a short-order cook, computer expert, and desk manager all in one perky little package. Nothing about me fits that description. Again I offer to work for free while I train, but she's not interested.

My last stop, and last resort, is the parks department, which is located on the ground floor of a two-story newish brick building on the edge of Manzanita Park, off the main square. When I enter the building, there is nobody behind the front desk. No bell to ring. So I stand and wait. Behind me is a large topographical map of Lithia and its surroundings. I study the streets of downtown, then my eyes wander to the hills and to the Lost Mine Trail. I hadn't realized just how long it is—the trail goes on and on. Stacey and I have covered only the first few miles of it. I'm wondering where the actual lost mine is when I hear someone behind me.

"Can I help you?" A receptionist has returned from somewhere and is standing behind the desk.

"Hi. I was hoping to fill out a job application for the parks assistant."

"I'm sorry," the woman says, not looking very sorry. "The position's been filled."

"Oh." I feel as though I've been in a different town all day, with none of the usual Lithia magic and good luck.

But then her expression changes, and she gives me a sympathetic look. "In a town full of outdoor nuts, these jobs don't stay open for long," she says.

"I guess not. Well, thanks anyway."

As I turn toward the door to leave, a young man in a dark-green parks department uniform barges through it like he's in a hurry.

"Cindy, you got those new flyers?"

"Hi, Doug. I got them printed up last night." She grabs a pile of large yellow paper flyers and hands them over. I can see the words BEAR WARNING in large letters.

"Great, thanks," Doug says. "I gotta get these up before the mayor returns from her trip."

When he leaves, I follow him outside and watch him climb into a Jeep. I hurry to catch up, then call out, "Excuse me! Doug?"

He looks at me as if trying to place me. "You don't know me," I say. "I'm new here and just have a question for you."

"What's that?"

"The Lost Mine Trail—is that one of the places where there have been bear attacks?"

He shakes his head. "I wouldn't worry about it. I mean, bears are everywhere here, but stay head's up, make a lot of noise, and you'll be fine."

Bewildered, I point to the flyers. "But what about those signs?"

"These?" He shakes his head. "Don't get me started." But he climbs back out of the Jeep and stands close to me, lowering his voice. "This is all one big enormous joke."

"What do you mean?"

"I'm sick and tired of everyone blaming these attacks on bears or mountain lions, or even Big Foot. You know, he's been spotted up there as well."

"Really?"

"Oh, yes." He shakes his head again. "And if there was a lake up there, you'd be hearing about the Loch Ness monster."

"So these attacks haven't been by bears?"

"I'm not saying animals don't attack people on occasion, but it's the exception—not the rule."

"Then how are these people getting attacked?"

"I have my theories." He lowers his voice even more, down to a whisper. "Bears don't attack people," he says. "People attack people."

I look at him. "Are you talking about a *serial killer*? In Lithia?" It doesn't seem possible in a place like this.

Doug gets an odd look on his face, like he's said too much. "I gotta get back to work," he says, and he climbs into the Jeep.

I watch him drive away. As I walk back to the studio, I find myself staring into the faces of the people walking through

Lithia, thinking that maybe I don't know this pretty little town as well as I think I do.

———ɷ———

David brings lunch for us at the store today. For the two of us, he brings mock-tuna sandwiches, made with tempeh and Veganaise. For Stacey, he brings a ham and Swiss, apparently by her request, which doesn't make him very happy.

They've both been on edge lately, and I think that's why her not-quite-veganism is annoying him. I know they've been arguing. I heard them last night, when the weather was surprisingly warm, my studio stuffy, and I'd opened my window, which faces the kitchen window of the main house. They were in there making dinner, and had cracked their own window. They were arguing over the food, which seemed to become an argument over something else. I heard her tell him that she's still her own person, that he can't change her. When their voices rose, it felt too much like being back in Texas, and so I closed my window and dealt with the stuffiness inside.

Around me, they act normal, though Stacey's been more distracted, forgetting things and forgetting all about customers she's in the middle of helping. I've been covering for her, bringing out shoes she was supposed to be helping a customer try on, or ringing someone up when she disappears. Yesterday, she said she needed to go pick up something at the drugstore and was gone for three hours. When David asked where she was, I didn't let on that she'd been gone that long. And when I told her that he seemed concerned about where she'd been, she didn't seem to care.

Now, Stacey is in the back room, claiming to be doing inventory, while David and I eat our sandwiches at the front checkout counter.

"What do I owe you for this?" I ask him.

"Forget it," he says. "I'll just take it out of your pay."

"Very funny."

"Don't worry, it's on me. To be honest, I'm just happy to have someone to share a sandwich with."

"Does it really bother you that she's not a vegetarian anymore?"

"They say a family that eats together…" His voice trails off. "It's only partly the food. It just makes you think, you know, when your values are so different. Especially when they used to be lined up just perfectly."

"Why did she give it up?" I ask.

"Who knows?" David's voice sounds weary, like this isn't the first time she's switched back. "She's someone who changes her mind a lot, even when it's something you don't expect. I guess I still haven't gotten used to it."

The door opens with a jingle of the little bell on it, and

Alex walks in. "Hi, David," he says, then looks at me and smiles. "And Katherine."

"Kat," I say.

"Right." He stands in front of the shoe wall. "Kat, I am in the market for a new pair of runners. What do you recommend?"

David nods me back to work and begins to clean up our lunch wrappers as I approach Alex. He is staring intently at the array of shoes.

I pull down a shoe and hand it to him. "These just came in," I say. "I like Brooks a lot. Recycled materials. No leather. Very breathable."

"That's good. Especially because I don't wear leather."

"Neither do I," I say, pleased to have something in common with him. "What size are you?"

"Ten."

I go to the back room, where I look around but don't see Stacey anywhere. I find the box of Brooks in his size and return to the front. Alex is already seated, his shoes off. I hand him the box and watch him put on the shoes. I find myself admiring his legs, the light, blond hair covering the fading tan underneath. My eyes travel up to his face, watching the way he presses his lips together as he pulls on the shoes, the way his ponytail swings forward as he bends down. He's so completely different from Roman, but still, I can't help but enjoy the view.

Maybe I'm a lot more lonely than I realize.

"Comfortable," he says, standing up, bouncing a couple times on the balls of his feet. "But what's up with the color? Why do men's shoes always use such garish colors? I mean, neon blue and red? And these lines of silver make me look like I've stepped off a space ship."

"I don't know why," I say. "Because men have no taste?"

"Why can't they just make these in purple? Or a nice, plain, old-fashioned green. Like the ones over there."

I follow his eyes over to the women's section of the wall. "I can get you a pair of those to try on, if you prefer," I say. "I'm not sure if they make them in your size—"

"That's okay." He smiles. "I shouldn't look down when I'm running anyway. Besides, these are going to get so filthy during my training that they'll be mud-brown within the week."

"You're training?" I ask. "Does this mean you're running Cloudline?"

"You bet. Are you?"

"I don't know. I'm still getting back in shape, building up my endurance."

"Where do you run?"

"The Lost Mine Trail. With Stacey."

His face darkens slightly.

"What is it?" I ask.

But he's already kneeling down to take off the shoes.

"Alex?" I ask, but he doesn't answer. So I add, hoping I haven't just lost a sale, "You can wear them out of here if you want."

"No." He straightens. "You can box them up."

"Roman!" Stacey's voice, from across the room, causes me to look up. I hadn't noticed the jingle of the door, or that Roman is now standing at the entrance, watching me and Alex.

Stacey goes right up to him and hugs him. "Where'd you hide yourself at the party the other night?" she asks.

"It's good to see you, Stacey," he says, ignoring her question. "It has been too long."

I don't like the way he is looking at her. Like they are old friends. Almost as if they are old lovers. Was she telling me the truth about the two of them?

"It's been *way* too long," she agrees. "We should hit some trails one of these days."

"Perhaps."

"So what are you looking for today?"

I find it interesting that, after days of leaving most of the work to me and David, Stacey is suddenly so interested in customer service.

"Just browsing," Roman says.

I'm now standing behind the counter with Alex's shoes, and even from here I can sense the tension between Roman and Alex, just like that night at the party.

"Hello, Alex," Roman says.

"Roman." Alex nods in his direction but doesn't look up as he pulls out his credit card.

"New shoes, I see."

"That's right." Alex hands me his card. Our fingers touch when I take it, and I hope he can't tell that my hands are shaking a bit. Something about being around the two of them is both intoxicating and nerve-wracking. It's as if there's a sudden, dangerous electricity in the air.

"Maybe they'll help this time."

"They're great shoes," I say lamely, as I swipe Alex's card and hand it back to him.

"That's not what Roman's getting at," Alex says. "He thinks he's faster than I am."

"I *know* I'm faster than you. As does all of Lithia."

"What Roman fails to mention," Alex says as he signs his receipt, "is that, unlike some shallow, self-important individuals, I am not obsessed with winning."

"Says the man who always finishes second."

Alex turns and takes a step toward Roman. "You want to go right now?"

"You already know what I want."

Stacey gets in between them. "Guys! Let's cool things down a bit here."

I have to admit, I'm glad she stepped in. And *cool things*

*down* is right—it feels as if the temperature has risen ten degrees in the store. I feel my shirt sticking to my back.

"I'm leaving," Alex says, and he turns for the door. Stacey picks up his shoes and follows him outside. Roman approaches the counter, and I busy myself with filing the receipt.

"I apologize for the scene," he says.

"That's okay." I look up at him. "You're an actor. You're supposed to make scenes."

"On stage, preferably."

"Details."

He smiles, the first smile I've seen. He's even more striking when he smiles. His whole face lights up, and I nearly forget where I am.

"Katherine, can I take you out to dinner tomorrow evening?"

I feel like jumping up and down, but instead I pretend to straighten up the counter. I'm a little self-conscious with David over on the other side of the store, folding running shirts, and I know Stacey will be back any minute. "I suppose that might be possible."

"Suppose? Might be possible?"

"Yes," I say.

"I'll pick you up at seven."

"You don't know where I live."

"Yes, I do. It's a small town."

I watch Roman as he turns to leave the store. In the doorway, he passes Stacey, nodding slightly, and then she looks across the room at me. I can't tell what she's seen or heard, but it looks as if she knows something is going on, or about to happen, with me and Roman. And she isn't very happy about it.

# Seven

The next day, not wanting to think about David and Stacey and what might be going on between them, I go out for lunch by myself. I sit in the cramped dining area at the Lithia Food Co-Op. The place is crowded, and I enjoy listening to all the voices, how different they are. People of all ages gather here, and in addition to English, I also hear people speaking in Spanish and French.

"Kat."

I look up to see Alex, wearing his co-op T-shirt and name badge.

"Hi," I say.

"Do you have a second?"

I nod, and he pulls up a chair and leans in. His eyes are a dark green, so dark that I'd mistakenly thought they were brown. They look at me with an intensity that I find very pleasing, though it also makes me a little nervous.

"I'm sorry for yesterday, at the running store," he says. "I acted like a jerk."

"You weren't the only one. Roman was pushing your buttons. Don't worry about it."

"That's actually what I wanted to talk to you about—Roman. I heard you have a date with him tonight."

"Who told you that?"

"It's a small town."

"Yeah, I'm starting to realize that." Had Stacey said something to him? Or maybe David? "I'm going to have to be more careful about what I say in public."

"I don't want you to go out with him."

"What?" I'm surprised he would say such a thing. "Why?"

"He's bad news, that's all. I don't want you to get hurt."

"I can take care of myself."

"I know you think you can, but—" He stops, as if unsure whether to say more.

Alex has no idea how much I can handle, or how well. "Look, he's gainfully employed and seems very well respected in the community. Given where I come from, that's more than I can ask for, trust me."

"He uses women."

I roll my eyes. "So? Tell me something I don't know about guys."

"I mean it," Alex says. "He'll suck the life out of you."

"So he's a little conceited. He's an actor. What do you expect?"

"That's not what I meant."

"Then what did you mean?"

He is silent. I can see that he's holding something back. But I'm not in the mood for his warnings, especially not for someone to play the role of big brother for me. If he could've seen me only a few months ago, he wouldn't worry.

"Alex, I hear you. But enough, okay? It's my life."

"Okay, okay." He lifts his hands as if he's going to back off.

"What is it between you two anyway?" I ask. "Why do you hate him so much?"

"Trust me, the feeling's mutual."

"I don't understand. Is it this whole competitive running thing?"

"Not exactly. But for the record, I could beat him at Cloudline. It's never been about winning for me. I'm just not as—as bloodthirsty."

Alex seems so earnest, and I like that he runs for the love of it, like I do. Suddenly I realize that even though Roman is the one I want to be out having dinner with, I'd rather be running with Alex. So I ask him: "If I try to run Cloudline, would you train with me?"

"Really?" He brightens.

"Really."

"You bet." He smiles at me and stands up again. "Well, back to work. I'll call you at the store sometime and we can set up a time to run."

"Okay."

I try to finish eating my burrito, but I find myself looking around the room, wondering if anyone heard us, wondering who might be watching me right now. Wondering who might come up to me tomorrow and say, *So, I hear you're training for Cloudline with Alex.* Today, for the first time, I'm getting the feeling that there is something different about Lithia, something that remains unsaid. I feel as though there's a secret here that everyone knows but me. I worry that it might be very important for me to find out what it is.

---

The knock on my door startles me. Normally, I can hear footsteps on the brick walkway that leads up to the cottage, like when Stacey comes by with food or to pick me up for a run. But I hear a dog barking next door, which is probably what muffled the footsteps.

I peek out the little porthole window on the door and see Roman standing there. I swing open the door. He is dressed in black, as usual, and I feel underdressed. I still have only one thing that's not jeans or running gear—the cotton dress that Stacey bought for me—and while I went shopping at a consignment store for decent shoes, I couldn't find anything that wasn't leather. So I'm still wearing the Brooks.

"You want to come in?" I step aside, holding the door wide open.

Roman takes a cautious step into the room.

"I'd give you the master tour," I say, "but the west wing is under renovation."

"Your maid's quarters as well? The help is apparently on an extended vacation." He is looking at the clothing scattered over the bed, mostly shorts and running socks. I did laundry that morning but haven't had time to put anything away.

"So I'm a bit sloppy. You're the bachelor—I can only imagine what your place looks like. By the way, where *do* you live?"

"Up the hill a bit."

"What street?"

"Why do you ask?"

"Because I've run on every street in town. I bet I've seen your house."

"I live on Highview Street."

"At the bottom, middle, or top?"

"Top."

"Near that castle?"

"*In* that castle."

"You live in the castle? The one on the corner?" I can't believe it. Every time I pass by, I stare up at it until I nearly trip myself. "It's gigantic."

"I like having my space. And I like the peace and quiet."

"Me, too," I say. "That's why I selected this cottage, for the space and the quiet." Then I have to laugh because now there's a whole chorus of barking dogs in the neighborhood. "I can't believe you live there. Every time I run by, I wonder what deposed king lives in that place."

"No," he says. "Just me." Roman's very serious, I'm realizing, not easygoing and quick to smile like Alex. *Stop comparing them*, I tell myself. *You're here on a date with Roman. Not Alex.*

"So why do you need a home that large?"

"Nobody needs a home that large. I'm renting it from a friend."

"Who owns it?"

"A deposed king."

"Really?"

"No," he says, his eyes showing amusement at my expense. Why is it that the only time he shows a sense of humor, it's at my expense? "It's owned by a wealthy acquaintance of mine who resides in the Balkans. I'm a caretaker of sorts."

"It must be one of the oldest houses in town."

"It is *the* oldest house in town. Built with gold money. Before people discovered the water, Lithia was best known for its gold."

"The Lost Mine Trail," I say. "I'm guessing that was a gold mine?"

He nods. "You've run it?"

"I'm just getting started. Where's the actual mine?"

"You'll never find it."

"Why not?"

"It has been sealed for years. Shall we go?"

Roman's dress shoes make sharp noises on the bricks as we walk to the street, and I want to ask him how he managed to sneak up to the cottage so quietly. But I think better of it, since I don't know him very well and he doesn't laugh very easily. Better to save my weird little questions, especially those that could be taken the wrong way, until at least the second date.

He stops when we reach the street and turns to me. "You look stunning, by the way."

"Thank you." Somehow, I didn't expect this. I've been getting the feeling, even though he asked me out, that he's not all that interested, that something's in the way. And to think I'm stunning in this dress, with these shoes, is a bit of a stretch—but still. "You're not so bad yourself," I add, a little shyly.

We stroll over to Main Street. I'm hoping he might take my hand, but he doesn't, though sometimes, when we need to make way for other people on the sidewalk, my shoulder brushes his arm. Though Stacey confirmed that he's the fastest runner in town, he walks slowly, and I find I have to keep restraining my pace. I tend to walk fast, always have. I don't like to walk slowly, to give people a chance to notice me.

But Roman doesn't mind being noticed. He seems to enjoy it, in fact. Women ogle him as we walk by, and a couple times I see them glance over at me as if to wonder, *What's he doing with her?* Roman nods to a few people, exchanges the occasional hello, all as if he's perfectly comfortable being treated like a celebrity.

"So where are we going?" I ask. As if I'm right on cue, he stops and opens a pretty glass door with the word Encore stenciled across it in fancy lettering. We're seated at a table near a large picture window, overlooking Lithia Creek.

"Have you eaten here yet?" Roman asks.

"No. I've hardly eaten anywhere but the co-op."

I look around. It's the nicest restaurant I've ever been to in my life. The place is about half full, and I can hear soft jazz music playing. The tables are covered with fine linen, and the candles give everyone a warm look, even Roman, who is strikingly pale.

I have to squint to read my menu in the dim light. Someone comes by with a wine list, and Roman orders a bottle of something I can't pronounce. I don't tell him I'm not twenty-one or that I don't drink alcohol—he doesn't seem to notice, or care.

He returns to his menu, retreating into silence. I'm wondering whether he's so quiet because he basically talks for a living, because his job is all about words and how he says them. Maybe he just likes to say nothing when he's not on the stage. I want to ask him, but don't know how. So I hide behind my menu.

Then I realize I've made a major mistake coming here.

I hadn't noticed when we walked in that this is a steakhouse. I see on the menu that there is seafood, too. But as I scan the menu looking for a vegan option, or even something vegetarian, I see nothing. Nothing but the house salad and a couple of side dishes.

It's actually not a problem to order a salad, with a side of roasted potatoes or Swiss chard, but of course the vegetables are probably slathered in butter, and I haven't eaten butter since I've been in Lithia. But what gets me is that no one ever thinks about the fact that vegans like to eat good food, too, that we don't just eat lettuce and hemp granola. Is it really so hard to come up with a faux-meat alternative to steak? A pasta dish that's not dripping with cream or accompanied by shrimp or sausage? I close the menu, not bothering to hide my disgust.

"Is something wrong?" Roman asks. "Have you found nothing you like?"

"I guess you could say that," I say.

He closes his menu and looks at me. "I don't understand."

"I'm a vegan. I probably should have told you earlier."

"Is this a recent development?"

"Sort of. I've been a vegetarian since I was eight, but lately, because of my—well, because I've been traveling a lot, I haven't been able to be very consistent. I mean, no one's perfect, but it's always been important to me. So I promised myself that as soon as I got settled, I'd become vegan."

"So since you've been here, you haven't had any meat, dairy, eggs, nothing?"

"Not since my first night here. And it's been really easy so far. I'm surprised there's nothing on this menu, in fact. You'd think they'd have at least one vegan option."

"It's a steakhouse, Katherine. That's what they do."

"But think about it—it's good business. Vegan dishes are a fraction of the cost of these steaks. A place like this could make tons of money off people like me who come in here with carnivores like you."

He gives me a tolerant smile. "I'm sorry, Katherine. I should have asked where you might prefer to eat. It frankly did not occur to me that you wouldn't like steak."

He sounds so sincere that I feel bad for making a fuss.

"Oh, it's okay. I should've told you anyway. I wasn't thinking."

The waiter returns to pour the wine. Roman swirls it in the glass, a deep, blood-red color, and takes a sip, giving the waiter an approving look. The waiter fills my glass, and I don't stop him.

"I have an idea," Roman says, after the waiter leaves. "Just for tonight."

"What's that?"

"Why don't you take a break from your diet? Try the steak."

"Take a break? This is not a fad diet, Roman. It's the way I live."

"But you said yourself that you're not perfect. Nobody's perfect. Besides, the cows are free range, grass fed. They don't suffer."

"Until they're slaughtered."

"True. But everyone dies sometime." I can tell he's trying to make light of the situation, the way many people do when my choice makes them think about their own, but I'm not taking the bait.

"The thing is, it's easy to rationalize anything if you try hard enough. It's free range. Humanely killed. Guilt free, right? That's what everyone wants—to eat meat and not have to feel guilty about it. But in trying to remove the guilt from the equation, you actually acknowledge that the guilt is there to begin with. And the only truly guilt-free meat is none at all."

Roman is now squinting at me, his eyes looking darker than ever. I've blown it, I realize; I've ruined our entire evening. I tend to get overly excited about this stuff, and now I wish I'd gone easier on him. No one wants to be lectured to, especially when they've gone to the trouble of taking you out to a beautiful restaurant, even if it is one that's not vegetarian friendly. I sigh, starting to prepare myself for an early end to what I hoped would be a long evening.

"That tree-hugger got to you, didn't he?" Roman asks, accusingly.

"Who?"

"Alex."

"This has nothing to do with Alex. I decided this before I ever met him."

"Katherine, runners need protein. I know this, and you should know this."

"I get plenty of protein. I get it from tempeh, tofu, nuts, bread, soy milk, vegetables, all sorts of foods. You should try it."

"Please." He looks as if I've just asked him to give up food altogether. Which is what a lot of people think happens when you become a vegan.

"Why not? It's good for you. Have you ever gone a single day without being a carnivore?"

"In a manner of speaking."

"What's that supposed to mean?"

He sighs. "It means no."

"Then maybe it's time you tried something new. C'mon. Why don't we both order off the menu, shake this place up a bit."

I'm trying to steer the evening back on track. I want to salvage it somehow. Roman is looking a little annoyed with me, but at the same time, it only makes him seem more attractive. Those furrowed brows, the dark eyes. The set of his mouth. I definitely don't want this evening to end too soon.

"What about Stacey?" he asks. "What does she think?"

"What does she have to do with this?" Maybe this isn't about my being a vegan at all. Maybe there is a lot more to these two than either of them is letting on.

"She eats meat."

"So? And how would you know that anyway?"

"It's—"

"—a small town," I finish for him. "I know, I know. Everybody knows everything about everyone."

"Evidently, there are still a few things I do not know about you."

A waiter stands before our table. "Are we ready to order?"

I pick up a piece of bread from the basket. "This will do it for me, thank you."

Roman's eyes flare and he dismisses the waiter with a wave of his hand. "I like you, Katherine. I thought we had a connection. I asked you out so I could know you better. I'm not so sure we have a connection after all."

"What, because I'm a vegan? You're going to reject me because of that?"

"I'm saying that you are the first."

"Maybe this is good for you. Maybe you need to expand your horizons a little bit."

"Perhaps," he says. He begins to swirl the wine in his glass again, and I pick up my own glass and take a sip. It is strong and rich and really quite good.

"However," Roman continues, "have you ever considered the possibility that *your* movement is wrong? That humans are indeed supposed to be carnivores? Have you thought about how widespread vegetarianism might impact the survival of *your* species?"

I think I've heard him wrong, or else these two sips of wine have gone to my head already. "You mean *our* species."

"Of course I mean our species. I am just wondering where vegans fit in."

And all of a sudden, I am tired of defending myself. I am tired of trying to justify what has been so natural for me, ever since I was young. And I don't like the fact that Roman can't accept me for who I am.

"Maybe you'd be happier with someone like Stacey," I say, before I can stop myself. "Maybe you're better off with someone whose mind you can change."

And with that, I stand up. My napkin falls to the floor, and I pick it up and drop it on the table as Roman starts to get to his feet. "Don't get up," I tell him. "I'll see myself home."

"Katherine, please. I didn't mean to offend. I don't want you to leave."

"I don't care what you want." As I'm about to walk away, I pause and say, "For the record, Alex is a great runner, veggie and all."

Roman seems to brush this off. "He's never beaten me."

"Maybe he will at Cloudline. Maybe I will."

I'm out the door before Roman can respond. And then I'm on Main Street, walking home, as quickly as I can in the dark. I keep waiting to feel a hand on my shoulder, to hear my name shouted from behind. But nothing happens.

I look back twice, but Roman is not behind me. I'm a little disappointed that he doesn't find me worth following, worth chasing after. *It's just as well*, I tell myself. I know that this would never have worked. The fact is, while I'm angry that Roman wants me to change, deep down I would like him to change, too. Like David said, I want to be with someone who loves animals the way I do, who cares about the planet, who doesn't eat meat because he believes, like I do, that every meal really can make a difference.

But now I will never find out whether we might have found some common ground, or whether it wouldn't have mattered in the end. I ruined the entire evening before it began, making a complete mess of what could have been an elegant meal, a romantic night. I could have simply ordered off the menu and put my stubborn tendencies to rest, for a night. Just one night. I could have done so many things differently— not just tonight but so many other times.

I hurry home, aware of all of Lithia's shadows around me, of the sounds of the trees sighing as I walk past. It's as if they're sighing in resignation, sighing about me. As if they know, as I do, that I am becoming my own worst enemy.

# Eight

Today is my last day at Lithia Runners, but while I don't know what I'll do for money, I have to admit that it might be for the best. Since my date with Roman, something has changed between Stacey and me, and not for the better. She's never asked me about it, for one thing, and she doesn't even know it was a total disaster. But I definitely get the feeling she doesn't want me to be seeing Roman. Stacey and Alex both.

I want to ask her about it, but it's so awkward being around her now that I don't know what to say. I have a hard time with this sort of thing. After my mother died, I grew up in self-defense mode, and I sometimes think that this is the reason I have a hard time communicating with people on certain levels. That is, I don't really know how to be close to anyone.

Most of all, it makes me sad. Stacey no longer jokes around with me. We still run together, but when we lace up for our evening runs, she hardly says a word other than *You ready?* or *Let's go* or *Hurry up, it's getting dark.* It's as if going running with me has become one of the chores she does in the store every day.

As we warm up, Stacey dons a bright, neon-orange running cap and jogs in place for a few seconds while I stare at it.

"Careful," I say, attempting a joke. "You might disrupt air traffic with that thing."

She actually gives me a bit of a smile, then turns her head to show me the letter "S" printed on the back. "It's from David," she says. "He wanted to personalize it, as if anyone else would be caught dead in it. It's a little peace offering."

"A peace offering?" I ask, but Stacey abruptly turns cold again.

"Come on, let's go."

Stacey and Alex both warning me about Roman seems to be some sort of jealousy thing. I understand it with Alex, since he's already asked me out. But Stacey? Despite their recent squabbles, I can tell that she adores David, and David loves her. I don't know why she would care who Roman goes out with at all. Unless she still has feelings for him. Or unless it's me she doesn't want him going out with.

Or unless Roman has some hold on her that she has not been able to break free of after all these years.

I can see that, I really can. Even though I walked out on my date with Roman, I still like him. I still want another chance. There is definitely something different about him. The strangely eloquent way he speaks. But then, he's an actor and he does a lot of Shakespeare. His silence. The way he looks at me, a lustful yet confident and knowing look, like I am his already, even though I am anything but.

When Stacey spoke to him that day in the store, he studied her with a similar intensity, but his eyes didn't linger on her. His gaze was a little dismissive, as if to let her know he had moved on.

Moved on to me.

I can't blame her for being upset. I arrived out of nowhere, and in return for her generosity, I appear to be stealing the attention of the number one bachelor in Lithia. The one she's saved a little place in her heart for. I should know better than to mess with something like that.

Still, I wish we could move on. I wish she would let it go, or tell me what's on her mind, since I don't even know where to begin. But that is not going to happen today. We're approaching the Lost Mine Trail, where, as we ascend, talking becomes impossible.

Stacey picks up her pace, cutting me off. "Hey!" I shout,

but she doesn't look back. I slow a bit, lingering behind her as I consider what to do. I want to just let her go on ahead, but on the other hand I'm tired of holding back. And I'm tired of feeling bad and not even knowing what I did wrong.

So I pick up my pace, and in less than a minute I am passing her. I can hear her breathing, pained, as I accelerate up the hill and around the bend. I should slow down now, but I don't. I'm feeling better than I have in a while, being able to run off all this bad energy. I feel stronger than ever, and my muscles are working beautifully, my lungs open and full. I'm feeling free, for the first time in a long while.

I hear a noise behind me. It sounds like Stacey shouting. She's angry that I passed her, and I really shouldn't have. I remember my promise to David. *Keep an eye on each other,* he said.

And so I turn around.

Then I think I hear a voice, or was it the wind? Then a piercing scream.

Now I am running full speed, racing back to where I'd passed her, the wind howling in my ears. I slide down the gravel path, tripping as I round a curve, then another. I must've gone farther ahead than I thought, or maybe Stacey had turned around and was heading back. She must've fallen, twisted an ankle or worse. I try to go faster, but the trail is unforgiving and won't let me.

And then I nearly trip on it—a running shoe in the middle of the path. Stacey's shoe. I stop and look around.

I pick up the shoe. There are drops of blood on it. So she did hurt herself—but if that's the case, then where is she?

I call her name, spinning in circles on the path, looking for any movement in the trees, my ears strained for any noise. The evening light is fading fast, and my eyes can make out very little in the darkness of the trees. My heart is beating faster than it does even when running up this mountain, and I raise my voice, shouting her name.

"Stacey!"

I remember that time she snuck up behind me, and I'm beginning to wonder whether she's playing a trick on me, some sort of cruel trick to get back at me for whatever is bothering her. But it's not funny.

"Stacey! Where are you? Stacey!" I am screaming now, as loudly as I can, my voice tearing in my throat. I wait for a response. I hear nothing, the woods suddenly more silent than I've ever heard them. I call again. And again.

There is no reply.

Sweat stings my eyes as I look on the ground again, for signs of anything. I see something bright on the side of the trail and run over to see what it is. My body fills with dread as I lean down and pick it up.

A hat. A bright orange neon hat. With an S on the back.

# Part Two:
# The Hills Have Fangs

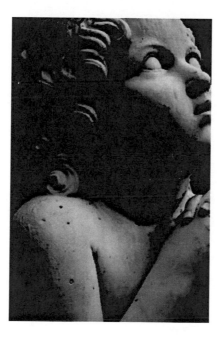

# Nine

It's all my fault.

David hasn't said as much, but I know he thinks it. How could he not? He'd asked me to look out for Stacey, and then I let this happen.

He was standing right next to me when I told the police what happened on the trail. How I left her behind, then rushed back after hearing her scream.

After I found Stacey's hat, I'd raced down the hill to the nearest house and pounded on the door until an older man answered. I screamed at him to call 9-1-1. I stood on the porch, my whole body shaking from the cold but mostly from fear, and the man's wife brought me water. I heard sirens in the hills below, growing louder and louder.

I called Lithia Runners and got the machine. Then I called David at home, and he answered right away. As if he'd been waiting.

I never should have left her behind.

I'd only been out of sight for a couple of minutes, but David had been clear about sticking together. So clear. I should have listened to him. I shouldn't have let my own worries get in the way, or justified running ahead of Stacey by the way she kept leaving *me* behind. Now, all I wish is that it were me who'd gone missing instead of her. I'm used to it; no one ever misses me.

But Stacey will be missed. David was very calm, silent as he listened to the police talk in hushed voices as their radios crackled. We stood next to each other on the dirt path as the search parties made their way through the trees. They wouldn't let us help—didn't even want us there at all—but it's a small town, and they knew what it meant to David. So there we were. Listening to the barks of dogs echoing down the valley. Watching the flickering beams of the officers' and volunteers' flashlights.

David said only one thing to me all night. "Are you cold?" he asked as we stood together on the Lost Mine Trail.

Someone had given me a blanket, and I had it wrapped around me, tightly, but I still couldn't stop my shivering. "I'm not cold," I said. And I wasn't, but my teeth chattered anyway.

Then they found her. Even before the police came forward to deliver the news to David, I knew she was dead. The radios they held went silent. Their urgency dissipated. And nobody made eye contact with us again. Not until the police captain asked for a moment alone with David.

The fog was thick by the time the police escorted me down the hill, the wind silent, the trees motionless for once. David stayed behind to escort Stacey to the morgue. The police took me home, and I felt like a prisoner as I sat in the back of the patrol car, the metal screening separating me from the two officers. But I deserved to be there. I left her behind, for just a few short minutes—but still I felt as though I'd committed a crime, a terrible crime.

The next morning, I looked out the window, up at the hills, and saw a layer of frost on the trees. Somehow I missed that last night, in the dark, all that frozen moisture whitening the trees, as if a blanket had been set down over the entire forest, like the blanket they used to cover Stacey's body.

And, like so many other things I've done, this is something I can never take back. I'll never have the chance to relive this moment, to do it over again, differently. This is something I'll have to live with forever.

———

I am back behind the counter of Lithia Runners. I showed up this morning, knowing that David would be in no condition to be here. I know I'm no longer an employee, but all I can think is that I am going to work here forever, with no pay, anything to make up for what I've done.

No one is coming in to buy shoes or running gear, but it's still a busy day. The news has spread quickly. By the middle of the day, at least a couple dozen people have stopped by, offering sympathy and flowers and food. The fridge in the back fills with casseroles and soups. I stick a note to each one, saying who it's from so David knows.

A few reporters call, some from as far away as Seattle and San Francisco. The police believe that Stacey was killed by a bear, or a mountain lion, and the reporters are curious. I hang up on them. Finally I stop answering the phone altogether. I listen to the messages, deleting the ones from reporters and keeping the ones from people David seems to know.

I get on the computer and read the news reports. The police said that Stacey had been dragged two hundred yards from where she'd been on the trail. The cause of death was apparently loss of blood.

I'm wondering whether I should've told the police what I thought I'd heard. But I'm not even sure I heard that voice anyway; it makes no sense. Even if it had been a voice, no man could have done what had been done to Stacey. No one was there.

I wish I had heard a voice. If someone else had been on

that trail, he might have done what I couldn't do. He might have saved her.

In the end, it doesn't matter. Stacey is dead.

I can't help but think of Doug, from the parks department, about what he said. *Bears don't attack people. People attack people.*

The police must know about the people living in the hills, the ones Stacey told me about. They must know what a bear attack looks like, or a mountain lion attack. I'm just a newcomer here. They know more than I do.

Then why do I have this awful, nagging feeling that won't go away?

I don't want to talk to the police anymore. Because it's a small town, and because I was with David, I'm one of them. I've been accepted, so far. But if I keep talking to the police, they might keep asking me more questions, like where I'm from and what I'm doing here. They might ask for a driver's license. Proof of identity. They might make calls. And then I might find myself in the back of a squad car again, not getting a ride home but a ride somewhere else. I might find myself a prisoner for real.

It has quieted down a bit, so when I hear the door open, I look up from the computer. Alex is standing there.

"I'm so sorry," he says.

I say nothing. There's nothing to say. It seems right to

thank him, but for what?

So I come up with, "Can I help you?"

He gives me a strange look. "Kat, I'm not here to buy anything," he says. "I'm here to see if you're okay."

"I'm fine," I say, and then I know what to thank him for. "Thank you for asking." I'm not used to people being concerned about me. It's nice, even though I know I don't deserve it.

"You don't seem fine."

"I am. If you want to help, find David. I haven't seen him all day." I don't tell Alex that I'm glad I haven't seen him. That I'm hoping I don't have to anytime soon because I don't know if I can face him. I think the guilt will overwhelm me.

"Okay," Alex says, reluctantly. "And then I'll be back to see about you."

I watch Alex leave, and I wish I had told him that I'm sorry for him, too. He knew Stacey a long time, and I've taken her from him. But I can't do anything to change what happened.

Day turns to night, and David does not come by the store. It begins to rain, and people pass with umbrellas raised. I envy each and every one of them, simply because they are not me. They have problems of their own, I'm sure, regrets and fears and second thoughts. But I would trade places with any one of them right now if I could. I don't think anyone has left a trail of regrets quite as long as the one I am leaving in my wake.

———⁓⁓⁓———

I close the store and walk home. Slowly. I know I have to see David, but what can I tell him? How many times can I say I'm sorry, and how many times can he tell me it's not my fault? Especially when I don't think either of us believes the other.

I walk down the driveway toward his house. *His* house. No longer their house. There is only David now.

The kitchen light is on. I walk up to the back door and knock. There is no answer. I look through the window and see him at the kitchen table, motionless, head down. I open the door and take a step inside.

"David? Can I come in?" He looks up at me, then back down again. I realize he is staring at the newspaper. The front page reads, in a bold headline: LITHIA WOMAN DIES AFTER BEAR ATTACK.

I sit down next to him.

"I know I should have stayed with her, David. I wish I could go back. If I could change anything—" I'm crying now, and I can't bring myself to look him in the eyes, not that he is looking at me anyway. He is still staring down at the paper. "I'm so sorry."

He doesn't speak, and I still can't look at him. As I stare at the paper, I see it darken with tiny circles, and I realize that they're tears. A moment later he puts his hand on my arm, and

I think it makes us both feel a little better, even though nothing has changed.

—— ~~~ ——

I sit on the side of my bed, too restless to lie down, let alone sleep. I've returned to the cottage after several hours in the kitchen with David. We both wept, and I made dinner, even though we weren't hungry. But we both ate a little, and as I was cleaning up, he disappeared. I heard him walking around upstairs, and that's when I put all the leftovers in the fridge and snuck back to the cottage.

Even if I could sleep, I don't want to. I can't bear the thought of seeing David every day, of receiving his generosity while I'll be reminded every moment of what I did. Of being the reason he is now living in that big house all alone. All because his wife was good enough to take in a homeless girl. He didn't even want to; Stacey had to talk him into it. And though he is being kind, I'm sure he doesn't want to see me ever again.

I know I have to do what I've done before. What I always seem to be doing when trouble catches up to me.

It takes only a few minutes to pack my bag and toss it over my shoulder. I leave the dress behind, hanging on the door. I pause for a second to look at it—so beautiful, the nicest thing I've ever owned. Then I turn away. I won't have any need for pretty things anymore.

I head for Main Street. In a mile or two, it will connect with the interstate, which will connect to points elsewhere. Points far, far away.

I'm suddenly eager to be gone, to flee this place and the horror of what I'm leaving behind. I pick up my pace until I am no longer walking down Main Street. I am running. Running, and running away—the only things I've ever been good at. And I just seem to be getting better and better.

# Ten

Endurance must be earned. It can't be bought or bestowed. As a runner, I've learned that endurance comes only through repetition, persistence, and pain. As a runaway, I've learned the same thing.

I realize, as I approach the entrance ramp to the highway, that I am losing my endurance.

I could run forever—this I will always know. But I'm not sure I can travel one more step.

Until I stopped in Lithia, I'd been seamlessly moving from town to town, my senses dulled to a life of hard beds, or no beds. Bad food or no food. Wet clothes or worn clothes. My endurance allowed me to deflect the taunts I encountered along the way. The rude people and the scary ones. If anything, I knew I could always outrun them. And I thought I'd be able to keep running forever.

But now I feel weak and cold and sad. I know I have to leave, but I also know that I don't want to. I don't want to start all over again. I don't want to reach the interstate, just a few hundreds yards ahead now, and to choose north or south. Seattle or San Francisco.

I begin to slow down, to delay my decision. After I left Houston, I realized exactly where I was headed. Lithia. The town I was born in. The town I remember from my earliest years. But now, I have nowhere left to go.

I feel raindrops. Perfect. Let it rain and soak me to the bone. Maybe this is the only way for me to rebuild my endurance.

Still not sure which direction to take, I decide to let fate make the call for me. Instead of choosing an entrance ramp, I will find a driver before I reach the highway. If the driver is headed north, I'll go north. If I get a ride south, I'll go south. I'm too exhausted to make the decision myself. The last decision, leaving Lithia, has been hard enough.

I stand tall and turn toward the traffic. I raise my thumb.

———

It's late, and the cars are few and far between. The rain picks up, and it isn't long before my clothes become completely drenched and stick to me like a second skin. My teeth won't stop chattering, and my raised thumb is shaking from the cold.

I've turned down three rides in the last hour or so, and now I'm wondering whether I should have risked taking them. But I haven't made it this far by being careless. The first two were trucks driven by scruffy, bearded men who just gave me the creeps. I've learned to trust my gut instincts, and I let them go. But I wasn't soaking wet then, and twenty minutes later, another driver pulled over, an older man who seemed harmless enough. He offered to take me where he was going, two towns north of here, and by then I was ready to escape the rain. Yet as I was thinking about it, he looked me over, told me I was *looking fine*, and I changed my mind pretty fast.

I know I shouldn't be out here at all. All the other times I've held out my thumb have been during the day, and I've only accepted rides with women or families. Even that is no guarantee of safety, but in smaller towns like this, it's easier to find people to take pity on a small-boned girl standing by the side of the road. I've never ridden alone with a strange man, and I don't plan to start, even if it means standing here in the rain all night.

And I'm feeling as though that just might be my fate when a woman pulls over in a VW Bug. I'm so happy to see her that I almost hop in before asking where she's headed. But she's only traveling another mile up the road, which would leave me nowhere in particular and too far from the highway, so I have to let her go.

By now I'm so discouraged, standing here like a wet dog, my toes squishing around in my Brooks, water dripping from my hair, my sleeves, that I don't even look over when I see, out of the corner of my eye, another car pull over. I can't imagine anyone who'd want me in her car at this point anyway, only to get everything as soaking wet as I am.

But the car idles next to me, and this makes me nervous. I begin to walk and it pulls forward. I glance over to see an ancient-looking Subaru, and just then the passenger-side door opens, as if to invite me in.

I'm wondering whether I should run when I see that the car is smothered in bumper stickers like SAVE THE WHALES and MEAT IS MURDER. Then the driver says my name. I bend down to see who it is.

Alex. I should've recognized him by his car alone.

"What are you doing here?" I ask.

"Looking for you," he says. "David couldn't find you, and your room was cleaned out. So here I am."

"You've wasted your time," I say. "Go home."

"Kat, please get in."

"I can't," I say. "Unless you're headed someplace far from here."

"Why?"

"Why do you think?"

"Is this because of Stacey?"

I say nothing. I feel the rain pelting my head and want nothing more than to get into the car.

"Kat, you can't blame yourself. Nobody else does."

"David asked me to stay close to her. And I didn't. After all they did for me—this is how I repay them."

"It's not your fault."

"I left her on that trail, alone."

"Suppose you were right there with her," he says. "Do you think you'd have saved her?"

"Maybe."

"Maybe not. Maybe you'd both be dead. Have you considered that?"

"I wish that were the case."

"If you won't stay for your own sake," he says, "then stay for me. I don't want you to go."

"Alex, please. Just leave me alone."

"I'm not going to let you run away."

"I'm not *running away*." He makes it sound so horrible, like this is even worse than what I've already done. And all I'm trying to do is keep from making things worse.

"Then what do you call this, exactly? You're hitchhiking in the dead of night in the rain. You're leaving David all alone just when he needs his friends the most. If you feel so guilty about this, after all he's done for you, then why don't you stick around and try to help instead of leaving?"

I glare at him, and I really hate him just now, mostly because he's got a point and I can't find any way to dispute it. Maybe he's right. Maybe I should stay. Maybe I should try to make up for what I did. But I can't help but feel that nothing good can come of my staying in Lithia.

"Just get in the car with me," he says. "We'll go back to town, and you'll get through this."

The rain has picked up, and I'm more tempted than ever to get into Alex's beat-up old car. It looks warm, dry, comfortable, and Alex is still watching me, leaning over the gearshift, waiting for my answer.

But I don't deserve his kindness. I step away from the car.

"Kat—" he begins.

And just then, a car pulls up behind his, stopping just short of the Subaru's rear bumper. It's a black, late-model BMW. Roman is behind the wheel.

He opens the door and steps out. He's wearing a slick black raincoat and doesn't seem bothered by the rain. He looks at me with those piercing dark eyes.

"It looks as though you need a lift," he says.

"Move along, Roman," Alex says. "This is none of your business."

"I wasn't talking to *you*, tree-hugger," Roman says, then turns back to me. "Katherine, you need to get out of this rain."

"What I need is to get out of Lithia," I say, taking another step backward.

"Very well," he says. "Get in. I'll take you wherever you want to go."

"Don't do it, Kat," Alex says sharply. He gets out of the car and in a flash is standing next to me. His face has changed, and he looks uneasy, frightened even. He reaches for my arm, but I pull it back.

"What's it to you?" I ask.

"I can't explain why," he says in a low voice. "Just come with me."

I look over toward Roman, who is standing next to his car. He doesn't seem at all concerned about Alex or what he might be telling me. "Well, you'll have to do better than that if you want me to go back with you."

"He's dangerous."

"You've mentioned that. And I've told you that I can take care of myself."

"Look, Kat, when I told you he'd suck the life out of you, I wasn't being metaphorical." Alex leans in and whispers, "Roman is a vampire."

"*What*?" I laugh, unable to stop myself; it's so absurd. And then I look at Alex, waiting for him to smile, to laugh with me—but he does nothing but stare back at me, his face completely serious.

"Alex, I don't know what your problem is with Roman," I say. "But you're being ridiculous. I'm not listening to this anymore."

Alex grabs my arm again, firmly, and I can't pull it back.

"I'm not letting you leave with him."

"Are you jealous, is that it?" I ask him. "You think making up bizarre stories about Roman is going to convince me to give myself over to you instead?"

"It's not that at all," Alex says. "I'm afraid for you. And you should be, too."

"This is insane. Let me go."

"I won't let go that easily."

"Let go!" Using all my strength, I yank my arm back and turn around, to walk back toward Roman, to his waiting car. But I'm surprised to find him standing right behind me, poised, on edge, as if about to take me from Alex if I hadn't been able to wrest myself away. Both men are staring at each other with eyes I haven't seen before. Both look as if they are ready to fight to the death. Over me?

It's all so strange, it's starting to feel like a dream.

"Come on, Roman," I say. "Let's get out of here."

I walk to his car, get in, and close the car door. The world goes silent. I've never been in a car like this before. It's like being in a house, with classical music on the stereo, warm air flowing from somewhere.

Roman gets in, and as he pulls away, I watch Alex in the side-view mirror. He's getting back into his own car, and I wonder if he'll try to follow us. But when Roman hits the gas, I can see that there's no way Alex will be able to keep up in his old Subaru.

I lean my head back and close my eyes and breathe. I hear a drip and realize that it's me, that I'm dripping water all over the seat, the armrest, the floor.

"I'm sorry," I say. "I'm making a mess of your car."

"It's nothing. Are you warm enough?"

"Compared to a few minutes ago, this is heaven." I slip off my shoes to give them a chance to dry. "Thank you for picking me up."

"Where would you like to go?"

"I'm not sure. I was going to go wherever my ride was going."

"Well, we're headed north," he says, and I look out the window to see the two white-starred lanes of the highway. "I could take you to Eugene, Portland, Seattle. I'll take you wherever you want to go."

"Seattle? You would do that for me?"

"Of course."

I can't believe my luck. After almost two hours in the rain, I have a warm, comfortable ride; a safe ride.

But then I wonder why he's so eager to get rid of me. Why,

after asking me out, he suddenly wants to take me hundreds of miles away from where he lives. And I can't help but hear the echo of Alex's words: *He's dangerous.*

"Do you *want* to take me all the way to Seattle?" I ask.

"It's up to you. Why do you ask?"

"I guess I'm confused, that's all."

Maybe I'm projecting, but he seems to know what I'm saying, and he reaches over and puts his hand on mine.

"Katherine, we're loners, you and I. We are fiercely independent, or, as some might stay, simply stubborn. I will honor your wishes because I know that I could not change your mind, even if honoring your wish is not my wish. Do you understand?"

"Yes. I do."

Suddenly, I am not so sure I want to leave after all. Not so sure I want to leave Roman behind. My head is feeling light, and I lean it back on the headrest with a sigh. "How can I stay in Lithia, after everything that's happened?" I ask aloud.

"You can stay with me. There are plenty of empty rooms in which to hide."

"It's all my fault." I feel tears welling up.

"You did not kill that woman, of that much I am certain. "

"I know. But somebody did."

"A bear."

"That's what they say. Sometimes I'm not so sure."

"What do you mean?"

"Oh, it's nothing." Then I decide to trust him. We are alike, after all, in many ways. Maybe he'll understand. "I thought I heard a voice. A man's voice. Up in the woods, right before."

Roman lifts his hand off of mine and returns it to the steering wheel.

"And there's this park ranger who doesn't think these attacks have been from bears."

A pause. "What does he think?"

"He didn't say." Now what I've just said seems as ridiculous as what Alex had told me just a little while ago. Serial killers. Vampires. Where do they come up with these things? Maybe there's something more in the water around here than lithium.

"Maybe he's just crazy," I say. "Maybe I am, too."

"We're all a little bit crazy."

"It's not that I want to leave Lithia," I say, sleepily. "I just don't want to make things any worse. To do more damage than I already have."

"Are you talking about Stacey, or our first date?"

I look at him, and he is smirking ever so slightly.

"That's not funny, Roman. Everyone loved Stacey."

"As did I," he says. "I suppose I view death a little differently than most. The cycle of life and death is not something we should fear more than we accept."

"Well, I can't accept it. Especially when it wouldn't have happened if I hadn't left her on that trail."

"Remember what Alex said. If you'd been with her, you might not be here yourself."

I haven't slept for nearly two days, and I feel my body crashing and rising, floating and drifting. I am drifting into sleep, on a tide so rapid I barely register what Roman has said. That he was not there when Alex said it. That there is no way he could have known what Alex had told me.

But I can't bring myself to speak; I am too far over the edge of sleep. What's left of my endurance fades into complete darkness.

# Eleven

I am on the Lost Mine Trail again…but instead of running, this time I'm flying, moving across the tree line, skirting the edges of mountains. White wisps of clouds cascade in front of me. I push through them and gaze down to open pastures and creeks and needle-sharp treetops. Then I notice something familiar, a trail snaking between the trees, following the curves of the hills, switching back and forth, descending the mountain. Suddenly I'm zooming in, unable to control what feels like a precipitous descent. And, just like that, the dirt trail becomes a river of blood, and floating on it like a raft is Stacey's neon hat.

I awake with a start, and it takes me a moment to realize I am not in the cottage. I'm in a strange bed. A huge bed. I spread out my arms and legs as wide as I can and still don't get close to the edges. I'm enveloped in white sheets, a white comforter; it's like sleeping in the clouds I was dreaming of.

Am I in Seattle? Or still in Lithia?

I look around the room. The ceilings are high, paneled in dark wood. The walls are white and blank, with only a lone painting hanging on one wall, like a museum between exhibits. The only color comes from the view from the large window on the left side of the room, a picturesque scene of trees and, I see now, the buildings of downtown Lithia.

I'm still here.

As I slide out of bed, I realize I'm wearing only my underwear, and there is no sign of my clothes from the night before. I discover a fluffy white robe on a nearby chair and slip it on.

I go to the window and look out, and that's when I get a better sense of where I am—very high up in the hills, in one of those mansions I run past on my way to the Lost Mine Trail.

I lean my forehead against the window to look around, and I glimpse a nearby house, its exterior all stone, in varying shades of gray, with a stone chimney and a balcony that disappears around the corner. I don't remember the houses being so close together in this neighborhood—and then I realize that what I'm looking at is not a separate house but another part of the house I am in. That I'm not in one of those mere mansions tucked away in the hills. I'm in the castle. Roman's castle.

I don't know how I got here. The last thing I remember is being in Roman's car. We were headed north. I don't remember telling Roman to return to Lithia. But maybe I did. Or maybe he read my mind. Maybe he knew all along that I wanted to come back.

I open the door to a long hallway. The floor is wood, with a Persian runner over it, and I look both ways before I call out, "Roman?"

But the house is silent. I turn away from the door, not quite ready to get lost by wandering down that long hallway. So I take a minute to look around the room. The furniture looks antique, and it is all large, as if this is a giant's room. The dresser's top drawer is at the same height as my head, and if I were to sit at the mammoth desk, I'd need a stepping stool to climb into the chair. The bookcase spans half of one wall and goes all the way to the ceiling. It's filled with old dusty volumes that look as if they might fall apart if someone tried to read them.

The room's only painting looks like something from an old European castle. I get up close to look at it, a portrait of some long-dead man, his pale face against a dark background infused with deep reds. The man's face is young and looks a lot like Roman's. He must be a great-great-something.

"Good morning."

I whirl around to see Roman standing in the doorway. He's wearing a silky-looking robe over what look like black silk pajamas, or very shiny, very comfortable pants. He always looks slightly overdressed, so it shouldn't surprise me that he dresses up to hang around his own house. Or maybe that's what people who live in castles do.

"Did you sleep well?" he asks, walking toward me.

I remember my dream, then quickly try to banish it from my mind. "Pretty well," I say. "I don't remember how I got here last night."

"I brought you."

"Obviously," I say. "What I mean is, I don't know how I got *there*, in that bed, wearing next to nothing."

Roman has an almost embarrassed look on his face. "You fell asleep in the car, and you were soaking wet. You needed to be out of those clothes."

I give him a look. "And who, exactly, got me out of those clothes?"

Roman smiles in that confident, flirtatious way he has.

"You?" I ask.

"I wish."

I'm both disappointed and relived. "Then who did?"

"Svetlana."

"Oh," I say. I'm not sure what to make of this. "Is she your girlfriend?"

"She's the maid."

"You have a maid?"

"She's my friend's maid. She came with the house."

"Oh." I can't seem to stop saying that, but this is all so foreign to me—castles and maids and a gorgeous actor standing right in front of me, as if it's perfectly natural that I've just woken up in his house.

"Would you like some breakfast?"

I am suddenly starving. "That would be nice."

"We have eggs, sausage…"

"How soon you forget," I say.

"We have toast, almond butter…"

"That's better."

He nods. "Come with me."

I follow him down the long hallway, our footsteps silent on the thick Persian rug. The whole place is so eerily quiet I want to jump up and down, make some noise. We walk down a long, winding staircase and through another hallway and a grand foyer that easily would hold my cottage, perhaps even a couple more. I get the vague feeling that we are being watched, but when I glance over my shoulder, I see no one.

We enter a gigantic kitchen. It's easily the size of the restaurant kitchens I've worked in, with all the commercial-sized appliances, only this one has fine cabinetry as well, and nice antique faucets. A heavyset woman is standing near the sink, which is large enough to bathe a St. Bernard in.

"This is Svetlana," Roman says.

"Hello," I say.

Svetlana nods deferentially toward me but says nothing. Roman speaks to her in another language, and she turns away, disappearing into a pantry that looks to be about the size of the running store.

"She speaks no English," Roman says. "Only Russian."

"You're fluent in Russian?" I ask.

"I'm fluent in a number of languages."

"Are you from Russia?"

"No," he says, and he pulls out a chair for me. The breakfast table is, like everything else in this house, old and huge. After I sit down, Roman goes to the other end, and we sit about six feet apart, facing each other like some old married couple in a black-and-white film.

I'm about to ask where he is from, if not Russia, when Svetlana returns with a tray. She sets down a plate with two slices of toast and a serving dish filled with creamy swirls of almond butter. Then she brings over a pitcher of orange juice and pours me a glass.

"Thank you," I say, in English of course, but she seems to understand.

"How is your toast?" Roman asks.

"It's delicious. Cruelty-free food always is." I notice that Svetlana hasn't brought him anything. "Aren't you eating?"

"No, I'm not hungry."

"I'd be happy to share my toast."

"Some other time, perhaps. We'll trade meals."

I sigh. "Are you still trying to convert me?"

"I might ask the same of you."

"Why shouldn't I? My diet saves lives. Your diet takes lives."

"Guilt is not a healthy emotion," he says. "It rots you from the inside out, turns you bitter. When you live in a world in which cruelty must be committed for one's survival, guilt is of no use."

"That's the worst defense I've ever heard. Especially since you can choose another way to avoid the guilt."

"I learned a very long time ago to leave that emotion behind."

"What's so wrong with guilt? It teaches us to be better human beings. Without it, we'd go around ruining the world and not think anything of it."

"And where, Katherine, has your guilt gotten you?" he asks.

I know he is talking about Stacey, but I'm not ready to talk about that. So I give him another answer. "Well, it's made me a vegan, which means I save the lives of close to a hundred innocent animals a year. I sleep better every night knowing that."

"You know what I'm talking about."

"I should get going. Thanks for breakfast." I stand up,

then realize I don't have the slightest clue as to how to find my way out of this house.

Roman has gotten up, too, and he's standing right next to me. "Have you ever kissed a carnivore?" he asks.

"I try to avoid it."

"Perhaps you should consider it." He moves a little closer, and I have to crane my neck to look up at him. Despite what I've said, I want him to kiss me, and I am hoping he will—but just then he steps away.

"I have to leave," Roman says.

"Now?"

"It's just an overnight trip. I've had it planned for some time. But you are welcome to stay here as long as you wish. I would like to see you here when I return."

I think of David, of his empty house. It's a fraction of the size of Roman's, but I know it must feel a hundred times as lonely.

"No, I should go, too."

"Where?"

"Back to my own place. To the store. David's going to need me."

Roman says nothing.

And just then I remember something he'd said to me last night in the car, as I was drifting off to sleep. "Roman, can I ask you something?"

"What is it?"

"Remember last night, when you said that Alex told me I might've been killed, too, if I'd been with Stacey on the trail? How did you know he said that to me?"

"I don't know what you mean."

"You weren't there when he said it. There's no way you could've known that."

"What I meant was," he says, "I don't know what conversation you're referring to."

Now I'm wondering about my sanity again. "You said I should remember what Alex told me. That if I'd been with Stacey—"

"Yes, I heard what you said just now," he interrupts gently, as if I'm a confused child. "What I'm telling you is that I did not say such a thing last night. You must've been dreaming."

"I don't think so."

"There is no other explanation, is there?"

"I guess not." But I'm almost certain he said it, and the way he's looking at me makes me think that he knows it, too.

Then Svetlana enters, carrying my clothes, dry and folded and smelling better than they ever have. I take them and thank her, and when I turn around, Roman is already gone.

# Twelve

We say goodbye to Stacey on a rainy Wednesday afternoon in Lithia Cemetery. The cemetery is on a hill above town, and I watch clouds scrape the tops of the ponderosa pines, creating a dark and gloomy canopy above us.

There are only a handful of us here, huddled under umbrellas. David wanted the ceremony to be small and private, so he made no announcements. There was no procession beforehand; there will be no gathering afterward. It's just this small group at the cemetery, just Stacey, family, a few friends.

And me.

The casket has been lowered. A priest stands at the grave and reads from the Bible. I can't bear to think about what's actually happening, about the fact that David will toss some dirt into this grave, and Stacey will be gone forever. So I let my mind wander in and out of the moment. The air smells fresh with rain and pine needles, and when I close my eyes I am back on the trail, alone, back when I used to love being there, when it was my respite, my escape.

Now, there is no escape. From what I've done, from missing Stacey. I think about the day I met her, how she was so kind, and I think about our last day, the look on her face as we raced up the trail, trying to outrun each other. She was trying to reclaim her place; she thought I'd taken something from her.

Roman.

There was something odd about her feelings toward Roman; it was more than a lingering attraction. He had a power over her, and somehow she'd been drawn back in by him. Enough to be jealous of me. Was it enough for her to reconsider marrying David? Was there more that I don't know?

Now I'll probably never know.

The priest is reading a passage from John:

*Amen, amen, I say to you, unless a grain of wheat*
*falls to the ground and dies, it remains just a grain*
*of wheat; but if it dies, it produces much fruit.*
*Whoever loves his life loses it, and whoever hates his*
*life in this world will preserve it for eternal life.*

I feel that this is true, that I am stuck in a place of eternal guilt, that there is nowhere else for me to escape. But I'm glad

I returned to Lithia. If nothing else, I can try to make it up to David for not keeping my promise to him. I can try to find out what really happened to Stacey.

A few days ago, an adult male brown bear was shot and killed. Just like that. Eye for an eye. The bear received his sentence before even having a chance—guilty before being proven innocent. And the bear was innocent. They conducted an autopsy that revealed no signs of a human within its stomach contents. How many more bears will they put down before they realize that it may not have been a bear? Before they realize that even if it was, we are punishing it for doing what it's programmed by nature to do.

No one is talking about what else it could be. David told me that the medical examiner who autopsied Stacey's body did not identify what caused the wounds other than "claws of undetermined nature." But there were no other telltale animal signs. No hairs. No teeth marks. And then there was the blood, or lack of it. If Stacey died of blood loss, where was all the blood?

I think this is why I have rivers of blood flowing through my dreams. I am looking for the trail that should've been there but wasn't. I'm trying to figure out, even in my subconscious mind, what really happened up there.

But the police and the media seem determined to keep the blame squarely on an animal. And no one is asking questions. Including me. But it's time for me to start. I owe David that much.

David now has a shovel in his hands, and I follow the small line to add a rose to the pile on Stacey's casket. David's face is blank, devoid of color, as he picks up a scoop of dirt and tosses it in.

These rituals today are supposed to bring closure. But for me, saying goodbye feels like a beginning. Because the only thing that I know will bring me closure is to find out who, or what, killed Stacey. And why.

People begin to walk silently back to their cars. I'm supposed to ride with David's parents, but I tell them I will meet them at home, that I need to walk. They nod at me, and I can tell they are somewhere else. Everyone is somewhere else now. Or trying to be.

I stay in the cemetery, walking away from Stacey's grave. I meander from there to another row, looking at every headstone, stopping to brush the leaves away, reading the names. Some headstones are elaborate limestone markers from the 1800s, with angels kneeling above, praying. The ones with lambs are children's graves. The limestone markers are melting away, even more so than the granite and marble headstones. Others are tilting to one side or another, tree roots having their way with them. Even in death, nothing remains static. Even here, there is chaos. Perhaps the only permanent aspect of death is death itself.

I bend down to brush away the leaves on one of the older headstones, and then I nearly jump back when I see it:

*Roman*

*B. 1836  D. 1861*

The headstone is so weathered, the letters so washed out, that I can't tell if this is a first or last name. But seeing the letters that spell out Roman's name gives me a chill. As if the name jumped out at me to remind me of what came between Stacey and me, how it led to that fateful moment on the trail.

Why can I not seem to escape Roman, even here, even today? Why do I want to be with him despite Alex's warnings? Roman seems to have the same hold over me that he'd had over Stacey. And that can't be anything but bad.

Roman is still out of town, or I think he is—I haven't heard from him. I look down at this old grave and wonder if it's a relative of his, or only a coincidence. I've assumed he's from some other country, but he's never actually answered my questions about where he's from. He's a mystery in so many ways, and it seems as if he wants to keep it that way.

I keep walking, feeling the squish of wet earth under my once-new running shoes, soaked again with rain, splattered with mud and grass. They were so beautiful and fresh only a few weeks ago, and now they look like I feel—worn out, beaten down, ugly.

Row by row, I continue my walk. When I look up and glance around, I see that everyone else is gone. There's nobody here but me—me and the rain, a few noisy birds in the trees, and a few hundred bodies six feet under.

Finally, I see what I've been searching for all along:

*Elizabeth Healy*
*B. 1966  D. 1999*

My mom.

The tears that I thought I had used up on Stacey come back in full force. It's been eleven years since I've been here, standing before this grave, and I can't tell whether it looks different or whether it's me who's different. Already her headstone is tilting a few degrees to the left. The closest tree is bigger now. A few birds have left their marks on the gray marbled stone, and a vine is stretching a skinny arm around it from the back.

I kneel on the grass and rip out the weed. Then I touch the stone and lean into its coldness. I talk to her every so often, and I usually feel as though she can hear me. This is one place I've longed to return, as if by being back in Lithia I might be able to hear her talk back. I've also been afraid to return. I've believed since I was eight that if only I could be here, we could communicate somehow—and I don't want to find out that's not true.

But I'm here now. And I tell her, "I'm sorry I was gone so long. I miss you."

I wait and listen, but I hear nothing but the sounds of birds in the trees and the droplets of water off the leaves. I push myself back to kneeling.

All I remember about my mom's funeral was the police car that led us in our long, dark car through town, how I sat next to my dad and how we never stopped at any street lights. We sailed right through like we were special. Until my mom died, we were never special.

My dad always found it impossible to hold a job, so my mom usually was the one who kept us going. She taught English at the high school. She'd grown up in Lithia herself and never minded that we were just scraping by. She used to say, *Look around you, and you'll see what's important in life.* I'm not sure I ever truly understood what she meant. But I do now; she was talking about nature. She thought it was more important than anything else that I grow up here, where we could be near what matters.

When my dad lost the last job he had in Oregon, he spent all his time at home. He and my mom argued and yelled all the time. This was around the time I started running, to escape the noise. I began to run faster and farther because it seemed as though their voices stuck with me, that I couldn't outrun all that anger. So I just kept trying.

I used to pray that my dad would leave us. For years after Mom died, I wondered if God had heard me wrong.

She was walking in the woods with our dog one weekend, early in the morning, when she was attacked and killed by a bear. We never saw our dog again, and police assumed he'd been consumed by the bear. No one questioned her death back then, even though they never found the bear that did it. At least, I don't think they did. We left before winter was over, as soon as the weather allowed us to go over the pass.

I haven't been able to stop thinking of my mom and Stacey dying in the same way. Alone on a trail. It's certainly not unheard of—Lithia is on the edge of a national forest, after all, thousands of acres of unbridled wilderness. It's a risk you take to live in a region like this. Natural beauty brings natural risks.

I no longer believe that Stacey died of a bear attack, and this makes me wonder whether my mom did. Maybe it's because my mom loved nature so much that it's hard to believe it would turn on her. But there's something about this, about all of this, that isn't right. And I have no idea what that might be.

I stand up and look at Mom's grave for a few more minutes. I feel some comfort in knowing that she is at peace, that she and Stacey are both at peace. Wherever they are, I have to believe that they're in a better place than I am. As many times as I try to run away, I can never seem to change the fact that I'm still the one who's been left behind.

# Thirteen

Today I'm headed to the library, and David will be going to the store on his own. He said he needs to get back to work, to be alone on his first day there after Stacey's death. He probably isn't going to open for business, he said; he just needs to be there and see how it feels. He's thinking of selling the business, he told me, but it's a big decision, and he doesn't want to do anything rash. He has asked me to stay on, full-time, until he decides.

Inside the library, I find an empty computer terminal and begin searching newspapers for articles and police reports on bear attacks in Lithia. There aren't many, but when I find them, I note the date and location in a small notebook. Then I look for missing runaways reported in Lithia, or even missing tourists. I also note names, dates, and locations.

I do this for hours, until my back begins to ache and my

eyes are strained and blurry. But I think I have enough to go on. I log off and take my notes to the main room, where I sit in one of the soft chairs near the windows.

Because my eyes are so tired, I take a few minutes to look around and reminisce. The library is in an old, one-story granite structure dating back to the 1800s—I remember coming here as a little girl. As I have grown, the library has grown, too. The old building is still here—it's where I'm sitting now—but it's been expanded, now connected to a vaulted two-story building.

My mom used to bring me here often, and I'd sit on the thin carpet and read picture books while she sat at a table and graded papers or read books. I never knew what she read, just that my dad criticized her whenever she brought books home, as if she was getting too smart for him. So she started reading at the library, away from the house.

I close my mind off from my memories and turn to my notes, flipping the pages, trying to piece these bits of information together into something that makes sense. Eventually, a picture emerges—and it isn't a pretty one.

I discover that there have been three fatal bear attacks in Lithia over the past five years. The attacks all happened deep in the woods, on the trails above the town, and three of the victims were young women. In all three cases, the cause of death was blood loss. And in all three cases, there were no witnesses, only bodies.

What is even more disturbing is the number of people who have gone missing in this area—more than twenty in the past five years. They are mostly women and mostly young, like me. The one difference is that these young women have family who come looking for them.

The feeling of dread that has been with me since Stacey died seems to deepen. What if I had been the target all along, not Stacey? What if it really should have been me instead?

I return to the computer and begin a new search: *serial killer Lithia.*

I get only one result. It's an interview with police based on "rumors" of a killer high in the hills. The police told the reporter that it's an unsubstantiated rumor, that people should not spread fear and panic.

But a parks department official claims it is not a rumor at all. His name is Doug Gibson.

—∿∿—

At the parks department office, I'm told Doug is clearing a trail in Manzanita Park. It's the same park I wandered into that first night, where I saw that warning sign about bears. The park follows Lithia Creek high into the hills, and while it was so much scarier that night I arrived in town, I've jogged there many times and have come to love it. Once you get a mile or so in, the tourists disappear, and the only sounds you hear are from the water. The ducks hang out along the creek, standing on rocks or swimming in eddies; the deer trot through the brush nibbling on everything in sight. It's beautiful during the day, but I'm always careful to leave well before sunset.

When I locate Doug, he has a chainsaw in his hands. I keep my distance, waving at him to get his attention. He's apparently dicing a tree trunk that had fallen across a walking trail.

When he sees me waving my arms, he shuts off the chainsaw and looks at me expectantly.

"Do you have a sec?" I ask.

"Sure," he says, eyeing me curiously. "Have we met?"

"Briefly. My name's Kat. I was in the park office, asking you about the bear attack."

"Right. The *bear* attack." I watch him crinkle his nose.

"Actually, that's what I wanted to ask you about now. I did some research of my own. And I agree with you."

"Agree? About what?"

"I don't think it was a bear either."

Doug looks at me suspiciously. "What kind of research are you talking about?"

"Internet. Old newspapers. Nothing more."

"Why are you so interested?"

"Stacey was my friend. I was there the night she was killed. I need to find out the truth."

"The truth?" Doug laughs to himself, then stops when he catches my eye. I must look angry or pitiful, or both, because his face turns serious and he studies me for a minute. Then he looks around, eyeing a teenage couple, hand-in-hand, walking toward us on the path.

"Let's get off this trail," he says.

He's a bit of an odd guy, and though I'm not sure it's a good idea, I follow him for a few hundred yards as he leads me past dense brush until he stops at the creek. Then he turns to me. His face is clean-shaven and round, which makes him look young and somehow a little innocent. He's solidly built and clearly fit, judging by the way he handled that chainsaw as if it were nothing more than a butter knife. The brush covers us from the sight of the trail, and I start talking, partly out of nervousness.

"Why all the secrecy?" I ask, motioning around me, showing him how isolated we are right now.

"Small town. Tourist-based town. They don't like it when I disagree with the cops. Bear attacks are just fine with city hall and the business community, so long as they keep tourists out of the woods and in town, shopping and going to the theater."

"If it's not a bear," I say, lowering my voice as much as I can given the rush of creek, "then what is it?"

"You mean *who*."

"So you think it's a person?"

He nods. "You probably read that article I was quoted in a while back. First and last time I was ever asked to comment, by the way."

"The one about the serial killer?"

"Nearly got me fired," he says. "And it did get me suspended for a month. And that was only for *talking out of turn*, as they called it. The truth is, I started that rumor."

"You?" I stare at him. "Why would you do that?"

"Because something had to be done. Someone needed to start paying attention. After that article came out, the FBI showed up with their high-tech equipment. They asked all kinds of questions and brought in their own experts to study the body of the victim."

"What did they find?"

"Apparently nothing. They said a human couldn't have done that. That was it. They didn't look one bit further, just packed up all their expensive gear and moved on to some other crime scene." He shakes his head. "Our taxpayer dollars at work."

"I'm confused," I say. "If it's not an animal and it's not a human, then what is it?"

Doug begins to speak, then stops.

"What is it?"

"No. Nothing good ever comes from me opening my mouth. And I need my job."

"It's okay, Doug. You can trust me."

"It'll only sound like crazy talk to you. It won't amount to anything, and you'll get all freaked out."

"I don't freak out easily," I tell him. "And I won't tell anyone that I even spoke to you."

"You promise?"

"Yes."

"I'm serious about that. I'm about this close from getting eighty-sixed from this job as it is, not to mention chased out of town by pitchfork-wielding villagers."

"I won't tell a soul. I promise, really."

He looks at me, still doubtful, then seems to relent. "Okay, here goes. Since you're already into research, you might want to get off the Internet and start cracking open a few books. Old ones, from back in the days of the founding of Lithia. You'll find stories about ..." His voice trails off.

"About what?"

"About ghosts."

"So?" I'm beginning to think maybe Doug is a little crazy. "Every town has ghost stories."

"And vampires."

I stare at him, feeling a sudden chill. I'm waiting for a smile or some sign that he's joking. But he's not, not at all.

"Some of the old-timers will tell you stories," Doug continues. "Stories passed down from their parents and grandparents. Seems to have started up around the time the gold deposits were all played out and the miners abandoned Lithia, leaving behind empty homes and bankrupt businesses. They used to say the vampires lived up in the Lost Mine."

"Near the trail."

He nods. "So there you have it, my crackpot theory. There are vampires in Lithia."

I hug my arms, still feeling that inexplicable chill. "Have *you* ever seen a vampire?"

Doug shakes his head.

"Has anyone you know seen one?"

"Nope."

"Any photos?"

"Why do you think I'm talking to you here by the creek?" he says. "If I had proof, I'd be the first to share it. The only thing I know about vampires is what I see in the movies, which means nothing."

"Then how can you be so sure?"

"Because there is no other explanation for these deaths. And you should know that, if you did your research. I know what you found. It's the same stuff I found. So you can't deny that I have a point."

He's right; I really can't. As ridiculous as it sounds, there doesn't seem to be any other explanation.

"I just don't know what to believe," I say. "It's just too—absurd."

He holds out his hand and begins a checklist with his pinky. "Well, there's always Big Foot—plenty of people in these parts have claimed to see him around here. There's aliens, though we haven't had any sightings recently; apparently they prefer the desert. After that, what else is there? Especially if this region has a history."

"But those were only rumors, too."

"You don't know that. Lithia is different, Kat. Don't tell me you haven't realized that yet."

I nod. He's right; I have. Maybe there are two sides to everything in life; maybe behind the magic of Lithia lurks something more sinister. I don't want to think about that, but it seems that this is the way of the world.

Doug and I walk back to the trail, where he starts up his chainsaw again as I start down the trail, back to town. I need to find Alex. I need to find a way to talk to him without breaking my promise to Doug.

# Fourteen

Around noon, I leave the store and head for the Food Co-Op on the pretense of buying David and me some lunch. I find Alex in the produce section, wearing a bib, unloading onions and garlic. I let a couple of shoppers pass, then I sidle up to him. Before he notices that it's me standing next to him, I lean over and say, "Were you serious when you told me Roman is a vampire?"

He whips his head around and stares at me, confused, as if for a moment he's trying to remember who I am. Then he glances around, takes hold of my arm, and ushers me outside to the parking lot.

"What's the matter?" I ask.

"I can't talk in there. Too many people."

"But you heard my question?"

"Yes. Look, I said a lot of crazy things that night. Forget

about it."

"You're the one who made such a big deal about it. What did you mean, exactly, when you said he's a vampire?"

"Nothing. I just didn't want you to get in the car with him. That's all. Forget I ever said anything."

"Are there vampires in Lithia?"

"Kat..." Alex glances around the parking lot, eyeing faces.

"Answer the question, Alex."

But he gives me that stare again, and this time I know what it's all about. Whatever he tells me, I realize, is going to change my life here in Lithia forever. And he knows it. That's why he isn't sure whether to answer me.

"I want to know the truth," I tell him, though I'm not at all sure I do.

"Yes," he says with a lowered voice. "There are vampires in Lithia."

"And Roman is one of them?"

"Yes."

"You're sure about this?"

"Yes."

"But how do you know?" I say. "I mean, if he really is a vampire, how come he goes outside during the day?"

"Vampires are a lot more adaptable than you think. Most of what you think you know about them—well, let's just say that most people really don't know anything about them at all."

I shake my head, and I look at Alex, hoping that he'll burst out laughing any second. But his face remains serious, anxious even. I remind myself that it isn't just Alex who believes this but Doug, too. Can both of them be completely crazy?

But then there are the bodies. And Stacey. And my mom. So maybe the idea is not so crazy after all.

Suddenly I have a million questions. "How many are there? Does anyone else know about them? And how do you know for sure about Roman?"

"Take it easy," he says. "Even if I could answer all your questions, I'm not certain I should."

"You have to, Alex. I need to know."

"Then go out with me," Alex says. "I won't drag you to some steakhouse. I'll cook you the type of meal you like, and we'll talk."

"How did you know about the steakhouse?"

"It's a small town."

"Is that all you have to say for yourself?" If I never hear *It's a small town* again, it won't be soon enough. "Were you *following* me?"

"What can I say?" He shrugs. "I like you, Kat. A lot."

"I knew it. That's why you're trying to talk me into thinking that Roman's some kind of demon."

"No," he says. "I'm serious about that. I always have been."

"If I'm in such horrible danger, then why don't you tell

me everything you know? How else am I supposed to protect myself?"

"You don't understand." He starts to reach for my arm, but I move away, out of his reach. "Come on, Kat," he says. "How about we just start over? You and me?"

"I'm leaving," I say. "I have to get back to the store."

"Kat!"

He calls after me, but I don't look back. I know he's got to get back to work, too, so he won't follow me this time.

I hurry away from the Food Co-Op, but as soon as I turn the corner, I slow down. I need to think. I can't believe I've just had a serious conversation about vampires. That I've talked to two guys who not only believe they exist but that they've hurt people. Right here in Lithia.

I understand now why people are so quick to accept the bear-attack story. Now I want to go back to believing it, like everyone else. It's the only explanation that doesn't leave you feeling like you've lost your mind. The way I feel I'm losing mine right now.

When I walk through the door of Lithia Runners, David looks up at me, as if waiting for something. I look back at him for a few seconds, then slap my forehead. "The sandwiches!"

David gives me a curious look. "You forgot them?"

"Totally. I'm so sorry."

"That's okay. So what did you get?"

"Um. Nothing."

He tilts his head to one side. "Nothing at all? You did go to the co-op, though?"

"I did."

"And you didn't buy anything?"

"I—I sort of bumped into a friend."

"But not in the checkout line, clearly."

"Um, no."

He smiles at me, the first smile I've seen in a long time. "I've been forgetting things left and right, too," he says. "It's natural, I suppose. Don't worry about it."

"I'll go back," I offer.

"No, that's okay. I could use a walk, a little fresh air." He puts on his jacket. "Tofu sandwich?"

"Thank you," I say, smiling back at him.

The bell jingles as he leaves, and I begin unpacking some new stock from the back room. The next time I return to the front, Roman is standing at the counter. The sight of him nearly makes me jump.

"Roman," I say. "I didn't hear the bell."

"Hello, Katherine."

I stand where I am, about fifteen feet away, and study him, thinking about what Alex had told me. I hadn't believed him before, so I've never thought about it—but now, I see Roman with new eyes. And even still, to me, he looks human, gorgeously human. Of course, don't vampires have the ability to attract? I think I saw that in a movie.

"Are you all right?" Roman asks.

I want to come right out and ask him, just put it all out there, no matter how crazy it makes me sound. I mean, why not? What's the worst he can do, kill me right here?

Actually, I realize, he can. The store is empty, the streets fairly quiet. Maybe I'd better take Doug's advice and keep my big mouth shut.

"What is it, Katherine?" Roman asks. "Is something on your mind?"

"Alex says you're a vampire," I blurt out.

So much for keeping my mouth shut. But Roman doesn't appear threatened, or even startled. He looks amused. And then he laughs.

"Alex says many things about me."

"Are you?"

"You're asking if I am a vampire?"

"I suppose I am."

He looks at me for a long moment before answering. "Yes."

I take a step back and knock over a display of sunglasses. They clatter to the floor in a pile, and I try not to step on them as I recover. "You're a *vampire*?"

"Of course." He smiles. "For Halloween, this Friday. I

always dress as a vampire. It's my favorite role."

"Oh." I feel like a complete idiot. I'd forgotten all about Halloween. David says that it's usually a big deal in Lithia, though the excitement has been a little subdued this year because of Stacey's death and everyone's worries about bears wandering the streets.

"That is what you're asking me, right?" Roman says.

"Um, yeah, of course," I say. To avoid eye contact, I turn my attention to picking up sunglasses from the floor.

"What will you be?"

"Me?"

"Yes, you."

"I don't know." When I think of where I've spent my last few Halloweens—serving drunk people whose costumes seem to give them permission to act like jerks—it's easy to remember why it's not exactly my favorite holiday. "I'm nothing. Halloween's just for kids."

"Not in Lithia. We take Halloween very seriously here."

"So I've heard." And I do have vague memories of Halloween. Being swept up in the parade in the thin October afternoon light. Trick-or-treating with my mom, walking hand-in-hand down dark and shadowy streets, never feeling scared.

"Everybody dresses up, you know," he says. "Everybody. For the parade."

"Not me," I say. "And I'm not much of a parade person,

anyway."

"Katherine, you can't live in Lithia and not go to the parade. It simply isn't done."

"Well, I don't have a costume, so there's really no point, is there?"

He smiles at me. "If it's a costume you need," he says, "I know just the place."

———ᨆᨆ———

Roman stops by the cottage sometime past midnight, after that evening's performance, and together we walk to the theater plaza. I can't help but think of Alex's warnings and wonder whether he's jealous or whether I'm truly not safe with Roman. A few places downtown are still open—bars and restaurants where the actors go after their shows—and that helps me feel more comfortable as Roman leads me down an alleyway to a black steel door. He takes a key out of his pocket and opens the door. Inside, it's all darkness. There's no way I'm going in there.

"After you," I say.

He takes my hand and leads me into a dimly lit, narrow hallway with concrete floors. As my eyes adjust to the light I can make out framed posters of plays gone by and old black-and-white cast photos. We pass doors that lead into rooms marked PROPS, TECHNICAL, SOUND, CARPENTRY.

"Are you sure this is a good idea?" I ask him.

"The only person taking a risk here is me, and I say it's worth it."

He turns into a room on the right and lets go of my hand. The room is pitch black. I stop and stand where I am, afraid to take another step.

"Roman?" I can't hear any movement. "Roman, where are you?"

Everything is quiet, as if Roman, too, is standing still. Or as if he's disappeared.

I raise my arms, reaching out to find Roman, or a wall, a railing, anything to give me some sense of stability in this total darkness. But there's nothing to grasp or to lean on, and I feel the room sway around me. I feel as though I'm about to fall over, when suddenly the room fills with dim light, which brightens gradually. I blink as my eyes adjust.

The room has high ceilings, and all around me are rows of clothing racks with costumes hanging from them. Along one wall is a long mirror and three doors that must lead to dressing rooms. But there is no sign of Roman.

I'm about to call his name again when I realize he's standing right next to me.

"Will you stop sneaking up on me like that?"

"I was not sneaking. I had to flip on the master switch,

which required finding the master switch. I didn't mean to frighten you."

"Never mind," I say. Then I look around. "So this is the theater's big closet."

"Yes, this is our costume department. This is the storage room for plays that aren't currently running. Everything from disco dresses to Elizabethan gowns can be found here. Now, as you'll see, you have no excuse not to dress up for Halloween."

"But these don't belong to me. I'm not going to steal a costume."

"You're not stealing. You're borrowing. I'll return it myself."

"What if they catch you? Won't you get in trouble?"

"I suppose I might. But as a lead actor, I'm willing to take that chance. Now, stop making excuses. Let's find you a costume."

"Well…" Still not convinced, I begin to wander through the rows of costumes. I have to admit I'm tempted by the idea of dressing up, of being someone else, even if it's only for one night.

I find a pair of overalls, large enough to slip on over my clothes. I pair it with a cowboy hat and boots.

Roman shakes his head. "We can do better than that."

"I like it. It's simple. Easy."

Roman holds up a long, slinky black dress. "You should

wear something to show off your feminine side."

I laugh. "I don't have much of a feminine side," I say. "I've always been more of a tomboy."

"A very beautiful tomboy," he says, which makes me blush. He holds up a wide-brimmed, pointed black hat. "This was from a sexy production of Macbeth we did a few years back. The witches were stunning."

"I don't want to be a witch," I say. I don't add that I feel dark and evil enough inside already, that I want to be something different for a change. Something more innocent.

I look through the clothes, amazed at the range of costumes, from bell-bottom jeans to nuns' habits to Victorian dressing gowns. The shoes and accessories are on the other side of the room, so as I try things on, I'm running from one end of the room to the other, feeling breathless the whole time. And having fun.

Finally, I find the costume I've been looking for. I hold up an Elizabethan dress that is so heavy my arm tires after only a minute or two, and I have to lay it across the rack in front of me. It's full-length, a rich dark blue with puffy capped sleeves. Underneath the capped sleeves are long, light-blue sleeves in a soft sheer fabric running down to the wrists. The neckline is low and square, and the dress cinches in at the waist. I take it into a dressing room to try it on. It fits almost perfectly, except that the skirt is too long and drags on the ground. I'll never be able to wear it like this, and I can't exactly have it tailored. I'm disappointed, but I decide to show Roman anyway.

When I emerge from the dressing room, Roman is standing there, holding some sort of device that looks like an animal trap. "This is what they call a farthingale," he says. "It goes under the skirt."

"Oh." I take it and step back into the dressing room. It takes me a few minutes to figure it out, but once I put it on and lower the skirt again, it puffs out wide, fitting perfectly, floating just above my ankles.

I open the door to show Roman.

"You are a vision of beauty," he says. "But you won't be able to wear your Brooks with this."

We cross the room to find a pair of shoes—pointy little heeled boots that lace up to the ankles. They squeeze my feet a bit, but they look perfect with the dress.

Roman leads me to the mirror and turns me toward it so I can see myself. The blue brings out the color in my eyes, and even with my hair pulled back in my usual sloppy ponytail, in the dress I somehow manage to come across as elegant. Standing behind me, he says, "You look—timeless."

I meet his eyes in the mirror. I find myself wondering whether it's true that vampires have no reflections, that they can't be seen in mirrors. If it's true, this means Roman isn't a vampire. It means he's human, and that these eyes now looking into mine are showing me something real.

Then I remember what Alex said. *Vampires are a lot more adaptable than you think…most people really don't know anything about them at all.* So maybe seeing Roman in the mirror proves nothing. Maybe Roman really is a vampire after all; maybe he's adapted somehow to make himself visible to me in this mirror.

It seems to me that there should be some hard-and-fast rules here. I need something to make it easy for me to know what to do. I need to know whether I should flee this room, run for my life. Or whether I should turn around, let myself fall into Roman's arms. Let him kiss me, which his eyes are telling me he wants to do. Let myself surrender.

But there are no rules—only the ones I make up as I go along.

I decide to turn around, into Roman's waiting arms.

# Fifteen

David is in the back room of the store, staring at a computer screen. I watch him from the doorway. I can tell his mind is wandering; he's been spending more and more time these days staring at nothing, lost within himself. But he has plenty to keep him busy: working, seeing friends, being invited over for dinner. He's got a lot of support, but I still hate to see him so lost. I know it will pass, eventually, but it makes me feel sad, and guilty. And I know we have to keep him going, to keep pulling him out of the darkness.

I tap softly on the doorjamb, and he turns around. "Are you coming to the parade?" I ask.

He turns back to his computer. "Stacey used to drag me to it. She always made me wear a costume. I didn't have a chance to get one this year."

"Let *me* drag you this time. I don't have a costume either."

I haven't told him about Roman's party. I'm still not sure I'm going myself, even though I said I would. I feel strange about going to a party so soon after Stacey's death, and I'm not sure about the costume either, though it's the only thing I have to wear. I'm definitely not wearing it now, for the parade, when half of Lithia will probably recognize it from one of the plays.

David's still sitting there, but he's looking less uncertain than before. "No one's going to buy shoes today," I say. "It might be nice to get out for a while."

He finally stands and shuts off the computer. I've already locked up the back, and we exit out the front. The parade is in full swing, moving down Main Street, past the store. We blend into the masses on the sidewalk, then find a little island near the square where we can stand and watch.

I can't help but smile at all the girls in their princess dresses, pink and sparkling, waving magic wands in the air. They're still at that age where they believe all their dreams can come true. I miss that age. You never get it back once it's gone.

I look over at David, and he's watching a group of boys in their Power Ranger suits. I'm guessing he's thinking the same thing.

---

Because I don't have a car and can't afford a cab. Because when David invited me along for dinner with some friends after the parade, I told him I just wanted to take it easy tonight. Because I waited until the last minute to decide whether I was even going to go to this party—these are the reasons I find myself walking up the hill to Roman's house on Highview. *Hills*, I should say. Very *steep* hills.

I can hear the party even before I crest the final hill and see the glow of lights from the castle. The deep bass of a song I've never heard rumbles through the neighborhood. I hope he's invited all his neighbors or that they're all out of town.

I'm wearing my Brooks because there's no way I could've made it up the hill in those tiny little boots. I stand on the porch to change shoes, then sit down on the large porch swing to lace up the boots. After my feet are properly squeezed in, I sit here swinging for a moment, enjoying being just beyond the life of the party. On the outside, where I've always been.

I try the front door, which is open, and walk into a crowd of priests, dead presidents, devils, knights, and superheroes. I don't recognize a single face. Actually, I can hardly see a single face; everyone seems to be masked, or hiding under very heavy makeup. I wish I'd thought to do the same.

I make my way through the crowd, feeling eyes upon me from behind the masks, from under the fake eyelashes. I'm self-conscious about my dress all over again—what was I thinking, that I'd be safer here than in downtown Lithia? Most of these guests are probably Roman's colleagues—actors, prop managers, stage directors. They'll recognize the dress and call the police. I'll get arrested, jailed, then sent out of town.

Which makes me realize that I should've left town in the first place, as I'd planned. Why hadn't I told Roman to take me to Seattle? Or had I, and he ignored me? That night is still a blur.

I duck into a shadow, a place where two walls meet, and lean back into the corner. I'm hoping no one will see me in my costume, or at least that Roman will see me first so he can give me something else to wear. People swish and clack past me, drinking and laughing. Having fun.

A man whose face is a ghostly shade of violet-white approaches, and I lean deeper into the wall and hold my breath, waiting for him to pass. But he doesn't—he stops. He's dressed in black and wears a black cape with a high collar and a deep, rich red on its underside. I squint at him in the dim light, trying to see if it's Roman underneath all that makeup.

"I vant to suck your blood," he says, with a thick European accent.

Definitely not Roman. I try to turn away, but then I realize that I truly have backed myself into a corner here.

"I am Victor," he says.

"That's nice," I say, my eyes flicking past him, at the other partygoers. "I'm looking for Roman."

"You must be Katherine."

"What's it to you?"

He laughs, his red lips twisting up his face. "Roman told me you were high-spirited."

"Really? Well, he hasn't told me anything about you."

"Perhaps you'll allow me to fill in the blanks?" He gestures toward the balcony. "Somewhere less deafening?"

I look him over. He's taller than Roman, and his dark hair has streaks of white in it, though this is probably part of his costume. He certainly plays the part well, with his formal manner, so much like Roman's, combined with that ancient-sounding accent. Something about Victor seems a lot older, but I'm guessing he's Roman's age. At any rate, I'm not eager to step out on a very high balcony with this very strange man.

"We can talk here," I tell him.

He looks amused. "You're afraid of me?"

"No," I say. "I just want to keep an eye out for Roman, that's all."

He takes my arm. "Roman will find you, my dear Katherine. I am certain of that."

And the next thing I know, he is propelling me out onto a narrow balcony—quickly, but somehow gently; I don't feel pulled or forced.

"This is much better," he says, "isn't it?"

The balcony overlooks the mountains, and the fresh cool air does feel good after being immersed in the noise and heat of the party.

"For now, I guess." I stand near the open doorway. "So are you an actor, too?"

"We are all actors in our own way."

"I mean, are you an actor at the theater?"

"I know what you meant. I am, like you, a civilian. I am in town briefly, for the theater, to take in the plays, the culture, to see how Roman is treating my home."

"So you're the friend who owns this place?"

He nods. "Would you like a tour?"

"I've seen enough of it already." I realize right after saying it that I probably shouldn't have. This Victor doesn't need to know that I've been here before, though he does seem to know a lot about me for someone he's never met before now. He's creepy, and not just because of the costume. It's the way he looks at me, or through me. I glance over my shoulder, into the pulsing beat of the party, and Victor doesn't seem to notice that I'm nervous. And he doesn't seem to mind that I have my escape route all planned out.

He's probably harmless, probably just one of those odd, socially awkward guys who never grew out of it. I can relate to that, as the tomboy who never grew out of it.

So I decide to give him a chance, and to find some

things out about Roman while I'm at it. "So how do you know Roman?" I ask.

"We met in Europe. A long time ago. I took him under my wing. He was—how shall I put this?—lost. Figuratively and literally. It was I who encouraged him to pursue acting. And it suits him, wouldn't you say?"

"Where does his family live?"

"He is an only child. Like you."

How did he know that? I don't remember ever telling Roman anything about my family.

"So he's from Europe?" I ask. "Where? Are his parents still there?"

Victor looks amused. "He hasn't told you?" He smirks. "I thought you two were close."

"He isn't exactly the chatty type."

"I didn't think you were, either."

"Only when I'm curious," I say. "So, where is he from?"

"You should ask him that yourself." Victor nods toward something behind me. I turn, and there's Roman. He, too, is dressed like a vampire, and I'm startled to realize that he's not wearing any makeup, that his skin is naturally so pale that he doesn't need it.

"What are you doing, Victor?" Roman doesn't look very happy with his friend.

"Having a lovely conversation with your girlfriend."

Roman looks at me, and we share an awkward moment, navigating around the word *girlfriend*. I can feel myself blushing as I remember our kiss from the other night. How I wanted to stay in Roman's arms forever. I remember thinking that maybe there *was* something special about Halloween after all, or at least the costume—I'd felt completely unlike myself in that dress, even more so than I do now, around all these other dressed-up people. In the costume shop, alone with Roman, wearing someone else's clothes, I'd felt free from all my worries. And beautiful.

"I apologize for Victor," Roman says to me. "He tends to feel proprietary over everything that crosses the threshold of this house, even when he has a tenant."

"And you, Roman, tend to feel proprietary over everything that crosses the border into Lithia."

Roman and Victor exchange looks that I can't interpret, and then Victor turns toward me and bows. "Until we meet again, which I'm quite certain will happen." He kisses my hand, then exits the balcony.

I watch him go. "So this is Victor's house?"

Roman nods. "He inherited it. Family money."

"He mentioned that you met in Europe."

Roman pretends not to hear my implied question and instead extends an arm. "Would you like to dance?"

"Dance?" I peek into the house, packed with people. "I

don't see anyone dancing."

"Not there. In the ballroom."

"You have a *ballroom*?"

Roman takes my hand and leads me through the crowd to a spacious room with an enormous dance floor, flowing with dancers in costume. A string quartet is playing on a balcony overlooking the room. The violins are electric, the music amplified and distorted into some gothic mixture.

I've never danced before. There were dances at my high school in Houston, but I was never invited to one. Besides, we were poor, and even if I'd been able to squeeze money from my father for a dress, I had no mother to help me shop for one, to show me how to apply my makeup, to teach me to dance. My father was useless, and I didn't fit in with most of the girls in my school—not the ones who went to dances anyway. I did have two friends, Kristy and Janelle, and we stuck together. Like me, they didn't fit in anywhere, and we would go to the movies on dance nights, hiding ourselves in the darkness of the theater, eating popcorn with fake oily butter and trying to remind ourselves that high school is nothing more than a blip in time, that we'd all move on. And we did, maybe too well; we're scattered far enough apart that I don't know where either of them are now. Sometimes I miss them. Like now.

I'm not sure what to do, exactly, when Roman holds up his right hand—but I take it. Then he puts his left hand on my shoulder, and I follow his lead. Not very well. I step on his foot. Twice. Then he stops.

"I'm sorry," I say, looking down at my Elizabethan shoes. "I'm just not used to these shoes."

He smiles, as if he knows very well that's not the reason. "Don't look down," he says, putting his hand under my chin to lift my face. "Focus on my hands." He moves his left hand down my back and holds me firmly. "Don't try too hard. Let me lead you. In fact, close your eyes."

Reluctantly, I do. He starts moving again, more slowly this time, and I can envision his hand on my back, guiding me. I grip his other hand in mine and focus on the music. As soon as I stop trying so hard to control my movements, to do it right, I begin to feel as though I really am dancing. No tripping, no stutter steps, just fluid motion.

I open my eyes to see him watching me. There is a glitter to his eyes, as though he is happy, as though he has me right where he wants me to be. And I feel that I'm right where I want to be, too.

But as much as I'm enjoying this, I wish Roman wasn't still such a mystery to me. "Why do I have to talk to Victor to find out anything about you?" I ask him.

"I suspect for the same reason," he says, "that I know very little about you."

"What does that mean?"

"It means we're alike. We don't like to dwell on the past."

"But we can't ignore it," I say, though I often try to do just that. "It's part of who we are."

"I'm an actor. I get to be many people inhabiting many different worlds."

"Is this why you became an actor?" I ask. "To escape your life?"

"When I play Hamlet," he says, "I *become* Hamlet. For those three hours, I am a man in a different country in a different century. My father has been murdered by my uncle, who then marries my mother, and I am coming to terms with the grief and the anger and, ultimately, I am following an irreversible path toward a tragic destiny. And as painful as Hamlet's life is, I welcome the brief respite from my own life. In the end, it is someone else's pain, not mine."

"What is your pain, then? Your life seems so perfect."

"There is much you cannot see."

"Why don't you ever show me?"

"Maybe one day, when you show me *your* life," he says, "I will reciprocate."

"May I cut in?"

We stop, and I turn to see Alex. He is dressed in a green-colored bodysuit with long pieces of bark glued to it, from head to toe.

"No, you may not." Roman glares at Alex, his expression

completely changed.

"Roman," I say, worried. "I don't mind."

"He wasn't invited."

"What's the big deal?" I ask. "The whole town is here. Just let him stay."

"Yes, Roman, let me stay. I made a costume and everything." Alex is clearly enjoying this little game.

"Alex, what exactly *is* your costume?" I ask.

"I'm a tree-hugger," he says. "I thought Roman would appreciate it."

"A tree-hugger? Or a sapsucker?" Roman says.

"You really know how to hurt a guy, Roman. How about you taking two steps back so I can dance with Kat?"

"How about I throw you out on your...bark."

"I'm not sure you could. Doesn't that cape get in the way?"

Roman nudges me aside, and he and Alex stare each other down, nose to nose. Typical idiotic men. I've seen this happen in bars from Texas to Oregon, and it's never any different.

"Come on, guys." I push myself back between them. But I'm so short, even in these heels, that they keep staring at each other over my head.

"Roman, Alex, seriously. Don't start anything. It's such a nice party." Neither of them moves, and I'm not sure what else to do. "Okay, how about this. Roman, let me have one dance with Alex. And then Alex will leave—right, Alex? What do you say? A win-win, right?"

Roman stares at me, as if I've just announced Alex and I are getting married. "A win-win?" he asks. "Hardly." Then he turns his back on me and walks away.

What have I done? Have I just picked Alex over Roman? I was only trying to make peace. Now I'm wondering why I did come to Alex's defense, even if it was meant to be a compromise. He's an uninvited guest; he has no business here. And he did rather rudely cut into our dance.

But the fact is, I didn't really mind.

I think I am drawn to Alex the same way I'm drawn to Roman, for different reasons. Roman is exciting and romantic, but as much as I like being with him, something about it feels dangerous. Alex is sweet and a good friend, but as much as I think he's not the one I want to be with, something about him makes me feel safe.

Why can't these two men be one, and save me all this trouble?

"Prima donna," Alex says, watching Roman disappear into the crowd. "Actors just can't stand to be upstaged."

"You could have waited until the song was over."

"I could've. But I'm tired of waiting for you."

Then I get that little flutter, the same one I felt just before Roman kissed me the other night. Alex's eyes have turned serious, and despite his ridiculous outfit, he manages to look remarkably handsome, long and lean as a tree. When he takes my hand, much the way Roman did, and we begin to dance, he moves as gracefully as the wind.

"That's quite a costume," I say as we move across the dance floor. I'm definitely not the best dancer out here, but I feel as though I'm getting the hang of it.

"I figure if everyone's going to call me a tree-hugger, I might as well embrace it."

"Why did Roman call you a *sapsucker*?"

"That?" Alex looks uncomfortable. "Oh, it's nothing. Hey, you're still a vegan, right?"

"Of course. Why?"

"I figured Roman would be trying to convert you."

"He is. How did you know?"

"He does it to everyone. Don't let him."

"Don't worry. I'm actually thinking I might get him to try being vegan. I think I might be able to convert him to our side."

"I wouldn't bet on it."

"Why not? Everyone is capable of change."

"Roman—" Alex stops, as if he doesn't know how to finish. "Let's just say he doesn't like vegans."

"That's a little extreme. I mean, I'm a vegan and he likes *me*, right?"

"It's more complicated than that."

"Then explain it to me."

"Well," he says, "I used to be like Roman. I used to think I was born to live a certain way, that my life, such as it was, depended on the death of others. I accepted this life as fact, but I was miserable. The guilt, I can't even describe it."

"I know what you mean. That's why I don't eat animals, either."

He gives me a sad look. "So I changed. It wasn't easy, but I did it. And now I threaten him. The *idea* of me threatens him. The idea of me creating others like me *really* threatens him. If every one of them becomes one of us, we would be the last generation. Granted, a long-lasting generation. But the last. Finality doesn't sit well with Roman."

"You lost me, Alex. Are you still talking about food here?"

He shakes his head rapidly, as if to clear his thoughts. "I'm just rambling," he says. "The point is, he doesn't have any respect for me, for my way of life. Or yours. And you have to be careful."

"If this is about the vampire thing—"

"Just promise me you won't change for him," Alex says.

"Of course I won't."

"Promise me."

"Okay, okay, I promise."

I see relief wash over his face, and I'm not sure why this is so important. But his features without all that worry make him look different—and it's only now that I realize his usual look is one of stress. I'd never noticed it before.

"Everything okay, Alex?"

"Sure," he says, and gives me a twirl on the dance floor as if to prove it. "It's just been a crazy time lately, that's all."

"A terrible time," I agree. I look up at him. I like his face this way, relaxed, happier. "Hey, when are we going to start training for Cloudline?"

"Anytime you want."

"Tomorrow?"

"You're on," he says, then twirls me again.

# Sixteen

Runners often say you need to put enough miles in the bank before you're ready for a race. Each training run is like a small deposit, one that doesn't just build up interest (endurance) over time but builds up confidence, too. And running, I think, is ultimately about confidence. If you believe you can finish the race, you're already halfway to finishing.

So I've been doing my best lately to put miles in the bank. And Alex has been helping me.

Since Halloween, we've been running every day. Alex doesn't take me up to the Lost Mine Trail. Instead we take a trail that leads up toward Mount Lithia, a trail that begins peacefully, meandering through Manzanita Park, then takes a sharp turn up the side of a hill, going steeply upward as it cuts back and forth, until you find yourself high above Lithia and wishing someone would pick you up off the mountain and carry you home.

But this hill is just a speed bump compared to Mount Lithia. The first time Alex took me up this hill, I was thrilled just to reach the top. Then he said, *Now the climbing begins.*

From the top of that hill, he took me onto a narrower trail, less traveled and more heavily covered by trees. And steep. Never-endingly steep. Every time we rounded a curve, I felt every joint in my body wishing for level ground.

Alex is a fast runner, and he tested me throughout. More than a few times I felt the urge to say, *Hold up* or *Slow down*, but I did not—partly because it took too much effort, because I was too winded to say much of anything. I let Alex determine when we stopped and turned back toward Lithia. And each day, he pushed us a bit further.

Miles in the bank.

This morning, I hear a low sound as I get out of bed. It actually takes me a second to realize it's me, that I'm inadvertently groaning as I try to heave my sore body out of bed.

I'm getting used to the pain, the sore legs, and I actually welcome it. It's not an awful pain, like from an injury; it's a dull pain that comes from my muscles being tested. From my body rising to the challenge. The weaker I feel after a demanding run, the stronger I feel the next day, and the faster I run the next time out. The pain is not unlike the dull pain over losing

Stacey, and it helps remind me that the pain will pass, that I'll grow stronger and feel better eventually.

I'm still sitting on the edge of the bed when I hear a knock at the door. My heart quickens—could it be Roman? I get up, before I have a chance to think about how frumpy I look, and open the door.

It's David.

"Would you mind opening the store this morning?" he asks.

"Sure, what's up?"

"I'm not feeling well," he says, and he doesn't look well either. I'm not sure whether he's really ill, or just sick in the heart, but either way it feels the same.

"I'll stay all day," I assure him. "Do you need anything?"

He shakes his head. I'll have to try to remember to bring food home tonight. He probably wouldn't eat much at all if I didn't remind him to.

I take a quick shower and grab a banana on my way out the door. It's not much, and I know I'll be hungry later, but maybe Alex will bring me some lunch. He stopped by with lunch from the co-op last week, and the other night he took me out to a vegetarian restaurant in the main square, where we ate portabella mushroom sandwiches with spiced curly fries. It felt far more comfortable to be in a diner-style restaurant rather than a candlelit one. And I could wear the running clothes

I'd worn to work. Everything feels so natural with Alex. What I like the best is that I don't have to fill the empty moments between sentences. We can sit quietly, and I don't feel anxious the way I do with Roman, wondering what he's thinking. It's what I like about Lithia, too. It's a place surrounded by nature, by silence, and people don't try to fill the silence the way they do in other cities.

Yet this is something I like about Roman, too. Well, that and his movie-star looks. He doesn't fill the air with empty words either. But his silence is of a different sort—it comes from someplace darker and lonelier and unexplored. I've been hoping I could be the one to explore it, to help open him up. That maybe he could help me, too. Our connection is so strong.

Or, it was.

I haven't seen Roman all week. Not since his Halloween party. I've been tempted to call him, but I don't know his number, or if he even has one. I've never seen him on a cell phone. Maybe it's part of his whole quiet thing, not being accessible.

I've considered waiting outside the theater some evening to catch him coming to work, or even later, to catch him going home. But most evenings find me heading up into the hills with Alex, so I haven't had the chance. Maybe Roman knows this. Maybe he doesn't want me to catch up with him at all.

And then I tell myself that though he was angry that

night, he doesn't need to hold a grudge. If there is anything between us, it should be stronger than one little dance with Alex. I try to be patient, telling myself that he knows where I live, where I work. He'll find me when he wants to.

But he hasn't. Not yet. And I wish he would.

Because the more time I spend with Alex, the more I enjoy it. The more I feel Roman slipping away.

---

There are two challenges to managing the store all by yourself: bathroom breaks and food. Fortunately, David lets me help myself to the energy bars we sell, as long as I keep track of what I eat. I've had three LUNA bars today so far. Not exactly the same as lunch, but they're supposed to be quite nutritious.

Getting in a bathroom break has proven more challenging. Every time I head toward the back, I hear the phone, or the doorbell, or both.

Finally I just have to ignore it all and take care of business. And, sure enough, from the little bathroom I can hear someone calling, "Hello! Anyone here?"

I race back out front to encounter a tall woman in bright-red racing tights and wraparound reflective glasses. She's holding a half-full water bottle and looking impatient, as if she's been waiting forever.

"Sorry," I say. "What can I do for you?"

"I'm in a hurry," she says, then walks over to the shoe wall and grabs a pair of Adidas. "Get me a pair of these in size nine."

I jog back into our storage room for her shoes, a little afraid of her. People this grumpy are a rarity in Lithia, especially now, here in the store, with Stacey being gone. It's been the opposite lately, with people coming in saying, *I hate to trouble you, but I need some shoes…*

And, wouldn't you know it, we don't have her size. I look everywhere, but there's nothing in a size nine.

I return to the front, where she's standing there literally tapping her foot. I resist the urge to tell her we'd probably have something for her if her feet weren't oversized. Instead, I apologize and offer to look for another shoe in a size nine.

"Are you kidding me?"

"I like the Brooks a lot," I say, then hold up a foot. "I love this pair."

She looks down at my shoe with distaste. I realize that the shoes have gotten pretty grungy, and I put my foot back on the ground.

"How many miles you run a week?" she asks.

"I'm up to about twenty," I say, rounding down a little.

"When you're up to forty a week, we'll talk," she says. "I've always worn Adidas. That's what I need."

She returns to the wall to scan the other shoes perched there.

"Are you training for Cloudline?" I ask, trying to make conversation.

"Yep," she says, dismissively, as if it's such a dumb question she can hardly be bothered to answer it.

"I take it you've run it before?"

She turns to me. "I've won it before. Three times."

"Oh." As she stares me down, I feel my competitive juices boiling. I feel the way Alex and Roman must've felt that night at the Halloween party. Like I want to challenge her to something. Not a fight. A one-on-one race, out on the street. Anywhere. Any length.

"I'm registered for Cloudline, too," I say.

She looks at me as if I don't stand a chance at completing the race. "It's not easy," she says. "Your first time?"

"For this one, yes."

"Well, good luck to you," she says, turning back to the wall. "I don't see what I need here."

"I can order them for you," I say, hurrying to the counter for a pad and pen. "What's your name?"

"My name is Erica," she says, "but that won't be necessary."

"Do you live in Lithia?"

"I live in California," she says, with a slight lift of her

nose. "I'm here to train."

"Well, it'll probably only take about a we—"

"Never mind," she says. "I'll just order online." She snatches her water bottle from the seat she's put it on and heads for the door.

I follow her to the door and watch her walk away. Now it makes sense; she's from out of town, and she doesn't know what happened to Stacey. It makes me feel a little better, knowing that Lithia is still the friendly place I thought it was.

But somehow, the encounter has made me feel a little less friendly myself. Not that competition is a bad thing—it can be a good, healthy thing. But all I can think of is beating Erica in this race. And not just edging past her at the finish line. I want to smoke her, as Stacey would have said. And I think that if Stacey were here, she would want me to.

# Seventeen

Someone is following me.

I am a mile into the Lost Mine Trail, and I keep hearing the crunch and shuffle of feet behind me. Yet every time I look, I see nothing. My mind must be playing tricks on me. This paranoia—it all started yesterday.

Yesterday, while I was out running an errand for David, I had that same weird feeling—that unmistakable sense that someone is watching you. So I crossed the street. And when I noticed someone else cross the street, about fifty yards back, I stopped to look at a window display, and this person stopped, too. When I turned to look at him, he entered a store, as if that's where he'd been headed all along. But I knew better.

Someone is following me.

I never got a very close look—but I could see that he's older, in his late thirties, and balding. He was wearing khakis and a button-down shirt.

After picking up what David needed, I stopped by the co-op to get our lunch. I felt as though I was still being followed, though each time I turned I couldn't see anyone. Either this guy got better at hiding, or he'd given up. Or maybe he had never been following me at all.

I found Alex in the cereal aisle. "Do you see anyone watching me?" I asked. "Look around and tell me what you see. But don't make it *obvious* that you're looking."

Alex looked around, unfortunately being very obvious about it. "We're the only ones in this aisle, Kat."

"Okay, then follow me." I described the man to him and led him to the produce section near the front of the store. I pretended I was looking at oranges as Alex scanned the customers.

"I don't see him," he said. "And besides, I recognize almost everyone in here. What's wrong?"

"I don't know." I look around, too, but he's right—that man is nowhere to be seen. "It's probably nothing."

"You sure?" He looked concerned. "Do you want me to walk you back to the store?"

"No, I'll be fine. So, are we hitting the trail this evening?"

"I can't," Alex said. "I've got inventory tonight. Love the overtime, but it's going to be a late night."

"Tomorrow, then?"

"Sure." He studied my face, as if he was reading my mind. "You're not thinking of running by yourself tonight?"

"Of course. I've got to keep getting the miles in."

"Why don't you just take the night off?"

"It'll just be a short run," I said.

"Well, stay off the Lost Mine Trail."

"But I thought we were going to run it this week," I said. Alex's training program includes three different trails, all of which will strengthen different muscles. A part of me was nervous about going back to the Lost Mine Trail, but I knew I had to do it eventually.

"That's right," he said. "*We*. Not you alone."

I felt my face getting red. "I thought you said bear attacks are rare."

"They are."

"Well, then, what are you worried about? Some other type of attack?" I stepped closer to him. "A *vampire* attack?"

"No," he said. "Of course not. I'd just like to be on that trail with you. What's the harm of waiting a day?"

But I decided that going back to the Lost Mine Trail for the first time was something I needed to do alone. I needed to be by myself when I went to the place where I'd last seen Stacey. I wasn't sure what emotions might overtake me or how I'd feel. And I think a part of me wanted a chance to say goodbye.

So here I am now, and the only emotion overtaking me

is fear. The trail is darkening quickly. It's been taking me by surprise lately, how soon the light fades in the evenings, as fall gives way to winter. The sun is already behind Mount Lithia, casting shadows over the trees. Wisps of fog drift between the treetops.

I hear another noise, to the right of me in the brush, and I freeze, listening. I peer into the bushes, straining my eyes to see what's there. The way noise carries here, it could be something as small as a lizard or as large as a deer. It could be a bear. Or a vampire.

But then the woods go silent again.

I decide to turn back toward town. Still nervous, my head turns at every noise, every sign of movement. I wish I'd waited for Alex. I wish that, instead of my teasing tone, I'd confessed that I do think there might be vampires here in Lithia, and that one of them might have killed our friend.

But I don't want to encourage Alex. What if he makes a connection? I think a vampire killed Stacey. He thinks Roman is a vampire. What if he jumps to conclusions? He already has it in for Roman.

And I still don't believe what Alex says about Roman. I can't tell Alex this, because of how I know. I know Roman isn't a vampire because of that night we kissed in the costume room. If he was a vampire, that was his chance to kill me—and he didn't.

Still, I'm confused. As much as I want to see Roman again, I don't think he wants to see me. And Alex and I are becoming so close. He makes me feel special in an entirely different way, in a way that maybe I like even more. Once, after a particularly fast climb up to 4,000 feet, he said, "I think you could actually win Cloudline."

It sounds crazy, but being told I'm strong makes me feel even better than being told I'm beautiful.

Of course, now I don't feel so strong. I try to pick up my pace, to get out of these mountains and back to town, but my legs are worn out. I slow down, then finally stop and walk for a while. I hear more sounds—creatures? other runners? the wind?—and start to run again, my fear overcoming my frayed muscles.

I've got my head down, focused on my feet, on putting one in front of the other, even as it's getting so dark I can hardly see them. I think of my mother. She wouldn't be frightened out here. She loved nature. She'd never been afraid of animals or anything else when she went out on the trails.

But maybe she should have been.

I tell myself to keep pushing, that I'll be off the trail again in another half-mile. I lift up my head to see where I am, how far I have to go—and then I see him.

I stop short. Standing in front of me on the trail, as if expecting me, is a handsome young man in a dark suit. It's so dark he could be mistaken for a short, branchless tree, and I blink to make sure I'm not hallucinating. But he's still there, looking completely out of place. This I never expected—a stranger in a suit. I'd have been less surprised to see a bear. Maybe less surprised to see even a vampire.

"Hello, Katherine," the man says.

I stare at him. Does the fact that he knows my name mean that I should be relieved, or more scared? The voice does sound familiar, but I can't place his face, especially in all this darkness.

"You don't remember me? I'm hurt. Though I was wearing quite a bit of makeup when you saw me last."

Now I know. "Victor."

"You're quite a runner," he says. "You almost had me perspiring."

"You were following me?"

"I was indeed."

I look him over, wondering if he's the one who followed me in town. As he walks toward me, I wonder how I didn't recognize him. He's got such a distinctive look, so tall and dark and intense—nothing like the everyday look of that balding man in town.

Victor steps closer, and I notice the glow of two alabaster canines overlapping his lower lip.

"You must really like your costume," I say.

"Pardon?"

"You may have taken off your makeup," I say, "but I see you've kept your fangs."

"These?" He reaches up and pulls on one. It doesn't move. "These, my dear Katherine, are real."

He takes another step toward me, and automatically I step backward, away from him. Doug was right, I realize with alarm. There are vampires in these hills, and I am face-to-face with one of them.

I try to match every step Victor takes toward me with a step in reverse. And I try to stay calm, which isn't easy. But I can't let him know that.

"So you don't just play a vampire on Halloween," I say, hoping that if I keep him talking he won't hurt me. "You're real."

"Very observant, Katherine."

He's moving toward me more quickly, and I'm having a hard time backing up at the same pace, especially since I'm scared to turn my back on him.

"Don't be afraid," he says.

"What do you want?"

"What does it look like? I'm here for you, my dear. Don't worry. It won't hurt."

I trip over a tree root, but I pick myself up right away and scramble backward a few more feet. Victor is moving slowly, like someone about to savor his first bite of food. Which, apparently, will be me. My heart is racing faster than it ever has during a run.

"Did you kill Stacey?" I ask him, the question popping into my mind suddenly.

"I've killed many people, Katherine. It's what I do."

He's closer to me now, but this happens so quickly I don't know how he got here. He's twenty feet away in one moment, and right in front of me the next, and he doesn't wobble on the unstable terrain. It's as if he's floating toward me, and I know that no matter how fast I run, I will not be able to escape.

But I run anyway.

I turn my back to him and sprint through a patch of trees, down to where I can re-enter the trail. And now I'm the one who seems to be floating—I'm running as hard as I've ever run in my life, not aware of the pain in my legs from just a few minutes ago. Not aware of anything but outrunning this creature who's close on my heels.

I'm waiting for a hand on my back, a pain in my neck, for something to clasp me from behind—but I make it to the trail, and I keep going. Maybe he's going to let me go. Could it be? Or could it be that this is all a set-up—a practical joke orchestrated by Roman? Or even Alex, to teach me a lesson?

I come to another turn, taking it fast, and nearly tumble down a steep incline. But I'm making progress. I can sense freedom.

Then I look up, and again he is standing in front of me. I skid to a stop and fall to the ground on my knees, my head at his feet. I don't look up. I can't. I feel him lifting me to my feet, and I don't resist. When I'm back on my feet, I look up. His face is now glowing, the fangs overlapping his lower lip.

"You killed Stacey, didn't you?" I say. "Please, just tell me. I need to know."

"Ask her yourself." He grabs my shoulders and opens his jaws, and I feel his body rising up to strike. I hear a hissing noise. I shut my eyes.

"Victor!" It is Roman's voice, and it hits us like a strong gust of wind. I feel Victor release his grip.

I back away, opening my eyes. Victor has his back to me now, facing Roman. Roman's eyes, like Victor's, seem to glow, with their laser-beam focus on Victor.

"Leave her alone," Roman says.

"You had your opportunity."

"It's not her time."

Victor laughs. "Roman, she is not a fine wine. You can't keep her on the shelf forever. She's perishable. You should enjoy her now, while she's ripe."

"I know what I'm doing."

"Playing games again is what you're doing." Victor turns around. He walks toward me, and I stand absolutely still as he steps behind me and puts his ice-cold hand on my shoulder. I close my eyes again.

"If you hurt her," Roman says, "I will hurt you."

Victor smiles, as if to taunt Roman. "Twice the pain. Twice the sorrow."

As fast as lightning, Roman leaps toward us, and then I feel Victor's hand lift from my shoulder. I spin around, and behind me, Roman has Victor up against a tree, his hands around Victor's neck.

"I'm serious this time," Roman says.

"Indeed," Victor chokes out through his constrained windpipe. "Indeed you are."

Roman releases his grip and turns to me.

I have inched my way to the edge of the trail, and I turn to look down, into a thick forest, onto a sharp incline. I know if I careen down this incline, I will find the trail again, but from here it doesn't switch back again for at least fifty yards of steep, dense forest. I will be scratched and bruised and broken and maybe worse. But it's my only chance.

Then Roman is standing in front of me, arms outstretched, prepared to stop me.

"I'm sorry you had to witness this, Katherine. This was not how I imagined things."

"So Alex was right," I say. "He was right all along. Why didn't you tell me?"

"How could I have told you?"

Victor comes toward us, rubbing his neck, which now has deep black bruises. "Roman, it is time. You know what must be done."

I can see Roman wrestling with some inner struggle—that same tortured look he often wears. It's a sad and haunting look, and I might feel sorry for him if my life weren't hanging in the balance.

"Why?" he asks.

"You know very well why," says Victor. "There will be others."

"Will there?"

"There always are," Victor says. But I can tell by Roman's expression that he isn't convinced. Victor is closer now.

"If you won't, I will," he says.

"Stop!" Roman holds up an arm, and Victor stops. "I need to think."

But before he gets a chance to think, I leap forward—and then I am in the woods, sprinting downhill at breakneck speed, wind howling in my ears, arms outstretched to dodge the trees. My legs can't keep up with the downhill trajectory, and I trip and roll downward, feeling branches cutting my arms and legs, tearing my clothes. I manage to catch myself, scramble to my feet, and keep running. I reach the trail, cross it, and lurch back into the woods to cut to the next switchback.

How many more until I reach the main road?

Then I hit a tree, and as I pull myself up once again, I see that it's not a tree—it's Victor, blocking my way. I let myself drop back to the ground, my head fuzzy with exhaustion. I'm not sure I even have room left for fear.

"Roman is weak," Victor says, looking down at me hungrily. "But I suppose love will do that to you."

He kneels, and I realize then that I am spent, that I have no energy left.

That my endurance has run out at last.

A part of me thinks that maybe it's meant to be this way. If this is how Stacey died, maybe it's the way I am supposed to die, too. Maybe it was supposed to have been me all along.

I see Victor's greedy eyes turn toward my neck, and his mouth opens, revealing his fangs. I watch him moving in, closer and closer.

And finally I give in.

I lean back, exposing my neck.

# Part Three:
# A Greener Shade
# of Pale

# Eighteen

I feel the damp earth under my body as I wait. A dark shadow hovers over me. And yet I'm strangely calm. I've accepted my fate.

But then, during these few seconds of waiting, I discover that I don't want to die. I am nowhere near ready for this—I want to live. But what can I do?

And then comes a bright light, a burst of energy. Like lightning without thunder, I sense the air change around me. Something's happened.

I look up and see that Victor is on the ground a few feet away, motionless. Above me stands Roman. He's looking down at me, the look in his eyes not unlike Victor's, and I'm too afraid to move.

Then he says, "Run."

And I do.

I sprint past him down the trail, and it's not until I reach the paved road that I allow myself to slow down. Looking behind me, I see that I'm alone again. No one is following me.

Still, I keep running, a slow, steady jog. I feel my lungs burning, my legs aching, but my body prevails, carrying me down the steep roads toward Lithia. I pass the yellow-lighted windows of the houses on the hills and wonder what their occupants know. Do they really believe there are only bears in these mountains? Or do they all know the truth, as I now do?

I run until I reach my cottage, and when my body stops moving, I almost collapse.

Yet I know that even though I'm no longer running, I have not escaped. I'm off the trail, but the horror of it is still with me. I turn and look back up at the mountains, wondering if Roman is still there. Wondering what he did to Victor. Wondering if they are there together, hovering somewhere among the trees, looking down on me. Looking down on their feeding ground. On Lithia.

---

I lie huddled in bed, too tired to move. But while my body is exhausted, my mind won't stop spinning. I sip water every few minutes, trying to rehydrate. I feel cuts and bruises on my arms and legs, even on my face, and I'm shivering from a cold that has seeped into my core.

I get up twice to check the lock on the door. But does it matter? After what I saw earlier, it seems that vampires can do just about anything; they can go just about anywhere they want to be.

Then I remember something from a movie—something about how a vampire has to be invited in. Is that true? Unknowingly, I have done just that. I've invited Roman into my little house. He has stood right here in this room, a few feet from where I'm lying right now. He could've done anything to me.

Yet he did nothing. Even tonight, he did nothing.

The room is growing brighter with the rising sun, and I close my eyes. Not to try to sleep—I feel as though I'll never sleep again. I don't know what to do. Doug and Alex were *both* right. Lithia's hills are full of vampires, and Roman is one of them.

It's a reality that doesn't feel real. Vampires come from books and movies, not idyllic small towns. Nothing I know about vampires seems to be true; they aren't supposed to go out in daylight, let alone play the lead in a Shakespearean play in a renowned theater.

Alex's words keep coming back to me. *Vampires are a lot more adaptable than you think.*

A knock at the door startles my eyes open. I lie frozen, wondering who's there. Is it Roman, waiting to be invited in?

"Kat?" It's David. "You awake?"

The room is awash in sunlight. I look at the clock on the nightstand and see that it's nearly ten in the morning. I'm late for work.

"Kat, are you in there?" David asks.

"Yes," I say, "I'm here."

"Is everything all right?"

"Yes," I say, then add, "No."

"What's the matter?"

"I'm not feeling well," I say. "I think I caught a bug or something. Is it okay if I stay home today?"

"Of course." He sounds a little doubtful, probably because I'm leaving him standing on the other side of the door. "Do you need anything?"

"No—thanks. It'll pass."

"I've got a bunch of medicine in the house. I can bring it over."

"It's okay, David. I'll be fine."

"Okay." I can tell he's worried, that he wants to see me, to be reassured. But I can't imagine what I look like right now, and I'm not about to open the door.

I hear his footsteps fade. The sun is shining directly into my face now, nagging me out of bed. I sit up, sore and miserable, and that's as far as I get. What is there for me to do? I can't go to the police, unless I want to be sent to a mental institution. I can't tell them one of the town's best-known residents is a serial killer of the most untraditional kind. I want to do something, to keep people out of danger, but anything I say will sound so crazy that it will only turn their attention onto me.

And that is something I can't risk.

I came to Lithia thinking it would be the perfect place for me. A place where no one knows me. Where I no longer have to look over my shoulder. Where the past can stay in the past. Where my secrets can be safe.

Instead, I am only gathering more secrets.

I let myself drop back down against the pillows. I want to go back to sleep, to wake up a day earlier and do everything over again. This time, I would choose not to go on a run alone. I would wait for Alex. I would—

Another knock on the door interrupts my thoughts. I sit up, trying to keep my breathing soft, though I'm beginning to panic. David is at the store by now, and I picture Roman on the other side of the door. Eyes gleaming. Waiting. Hungry.

"Kat?"

I let my breath out in a long sigh.

"Kat, are you there? It's Alex."

Just the man I need to see. But as I get out of bed, I find myself wondering if it's all a trick. Can vampires disguise their voices? I don't know anything anymore.

I tiptoe over to the side window and peek through the curtain. Alex, in his usual jeans and worn T-shirt, is waiting patiently. He's arrived as if I've summoned him—the one person I can talk to about all of this—but even as I open the door, I'm beginning to doubt myself. I'm wondering whether it's all been part of a long, strange dream.

I open the door. His eyes widen when he sees me. "What on earth happened to you?" he asks.

I've almost forgotten what I look like.

"You went running last night, didn't you?" he says. "What happened?"

I don't invite him in, but he crosses the threshold and goes into the little galley kitchen, opening drawers and cupboards.

"What are you doing?" I ask.

"We need to take care of those scratches before they get infected," he says. "It looks like you took a pretty bad spill."

"It could've been worse," I say. "A lot worse."

He finds a first-aid kit under the sink and sits me down at the little table. He uses a damp paper towel to clean the scratches on my face and my bare arms. His touch is gentle. "So," he says, "are you going to tell me what happened?"

"Vampires."

He's opening a tube of ointment and pauses for a moment before continuing. "But you're okay?"

"You don't seem surprised."

"I'm not."

"So you believe me?"

"I believe you."

"Why?"

He dabs some ointment on the cut on my face. "First, I know you wouldn't lie to me. Second, you're not telling me anything I don't already know."

"Well, it's certainly news to me. Who else knows about this? Have they been here all along? Why doesn't anyone say anything?"

Alex doesn't answer as he puts Band-Aids on the deeper scratches. I wait, and he bandages the scrapes on my legs as well. When he finally speaks, he surprises me.

"You want to get out of town for a while?" he asks. "I think we could both use a change of scenery."

"When I tried to leave Lithia, you wouldn't let me. Now, you want to take me away?"

"Just a day trip," he says.

"Where?"

"The redwood forest," he says.

"Are there vampires in the redwoods?"

He gives me a strange look, then says, "I'll wait outside. Get dressed and meet me in the car."

—∿—

I'm so exhausted, I fall asleep soon after getting into Alex's Subaru. Alex has that effect on me—not that he puts me to sleep but that he creates a space that makes me feel safe enough to close my eyes and relax.

When I wake up, we're on a narrow two-lane highway, deep inside a forest. The trees around us block the clouds, or maybe we're *in* the clouds—the small amount of sunlight that reaches us is brightened by a strange, ghostly mist.

"They call this the Redwood Highway," Alex says, glancing over at me.

I respond by turning away, leaning my head against the window, watching the trees flash by.

"Kat? You asleep?"

"How can I sleep if you keep talking to me?"

"Okay, okay. I'll stop talking."

I turn back to him. "It's not your talking that bothers me, it's what you're saying. And not saying. You're showing me the sights when you should be asking me about the vampires I saw last night. Or, more specifically, how I escaped having the blood drained from my body. Do you even care?"

"Of course I care," he says.

"Well, then, you're a better actor than our vampire friend Roman. Because you don't seem the least bit bothered."

"I do want to talk," he says. "Trust me, Kat. There's a reason I want you to be here when we talk about this. It will all make sense then."

"Nothing makes sense anymore."

I stare sullenly out the window. The road ahead is getting darker, as if someone above is turning the dial of a dimmer switch. I look up, expecting thick rain clouds, but instead I see nothing but trees—enormous canopies of dark green pine needles. The sky has completely disappeared. I look back at the road, which has narrowed quite a lot, hemmed in by gigantic, prehistoric-looking tree trunks. They emerge from the earth like bark-covered missiles, with no end in sight, even as I try to glimpse their tops.

"Welcome to the redwoods," Alex says.

I press my face against the window, trying to improve my view. "It's like looking at a forest through a magnifying glass."

"Pretty amazing, isn't it?"

I'd been impressed with the trees in the hills of Lithia, but these trees are at least five times wider and taller. Ahead, the road curves around a tree trunk as wide as a mobile home. I see a turnout in the narrow road and ask Alex to pull over.

I get out of the car and walk up to one of the trees. The ground under my feet is thick with bark and pine needles, and it's so spongy it's like walking on a trampoline; I practically bounce. I reach out and touch the tree, its bark thick and damp from the mist. I clasp a section of bark and hold on as I arch my back and look up, following the trunk until it disappears into wisps of fog high above. Its top is completely hidden in the clouds, and I wonder what it must look like from above—a bunch of green treetops rising from a blanket of white, puffy clouds. I slowly walk around the tree trunk on the springy earth. Everything is lush and green, the air so thick I feel it clinging to my skin and hair.

Alex says gently, "We're almost there, Kat."

Reluctantly, I get back into the car. After another mile, the weaving blacktop road turns into a one-lane gravel road. Alex has to slow down to nearly a crawl, and about ten minutes later, the road changes again, this time yielding to soft dirt. Large ferns brush up against the sides of the Subaru like a car wash.

Finally, Alex stops, and I step out again. While we'd passed a couple of other cars back on the paved road, that was miles ago, and there is no one else here. We are all alone.

"Follow me," Alex says.

He heads into thick brush, pushing large drooping ferns out of the way, holding them for me as though he's holding doors open. I follow close behind, breathing deeply the whole time, not from exertion but from the cool, clean feel of the air, rich with oxygen.

I notice that we are not on a trail; we're in the middle of this forest-jungle, and I wonder if he knows exactly where he's going. I want to ask how much farther he's taking me, but

I actually don't care if we have another ten miles to go. It's so beautiful here I could walk forever. It's like being in a cathedral of nature, ancient and sacred.

Then Alex stops and turns to me. "We're here."

I stop, too, listening to the sounds of the forest: faraway birds, the whisper of the trees, the slow dripping of moisture from the branches. "Where is *here* exactly?"

"Technically speaking, we're in Jedediah Smith Redwood State Park. Two miles from the California border. But I never really think of it by its formal name. For me, it's home."

I stare at him. "You were raised in the forest?"

He laughs. "In a manner of speaking. I brought you here to show you a friend of mine."

"You're serious? People really live out here?" It doesn't seem possible, given that we're now in a place with no roads. There aren't even any trails. But at this point, I'm past being surprised by anything.

"No, no one lives here. And this friend isn't a person. It's a tree."

"A tree?"

"Not just any tree," he says. "Most trees here are two hundred to three hundred feet tall. The tallest on record is three hundred and seventy-nine feet. It's named Hyperion."

"Does your tree friend have a name, too?"

He smiles at me. "Very funny."

I look around. "So where is this Hyperion?"

"Hyperion's location is secret."

"Why?"

"To protect it from tourists and the hordes who would try to climb it." He smiles again. "But I know of a taller tree, one that nobody else knows about."

"Where is it?"

"Right there."

He points to the tree in front of us. I look up to see the top, but, like the others, it is hidden in clouds.

"This tree is four hundred feet tall," Alex says. "Four hundred and one, to be exact. The tallest tree on the planet."

"How do you know?"

"I've climbed it. I've climbed most of these trees. This is where I come to relax. To get away from people."

"You couldn't have picked a better place." It's so beautiful here, so remote, that I've almost forgotten that there's another world out there. That the other world, the one I live in, is apparently filled with vampires.

"Alex, why didn't you tell me Roman was a vampire?"

"I did."

"I mean, why didn't you make me listen? And why didn't you tell me there were more?"

"You didn't want to hear it, Kat."

"Roman's friend Victor tried to kill me last night," I say,

eager to get the story out, to tell someone. "I thought it was all over. And then it seemed like Roman was going to kill me. But he didn't. It's almost like—he saved me."

Alex is looking at me, his face serious, almost somber. "He probably did. But that doesn't mean you're safe."

"Why?"

"It's complicated."

"What's complicated about it? You just call the police and stop them."

"So did you call the police?"

I go silent. I didn't, and I can't tell Alex why.

"You see, Kat? Everything is complicated."

"Well, you should've been clearer with me. I thought you were just jealous of Roman. I didn't know my *life* actually was in danger."

"You still don't know the whole story."

"Seriously, Alex? I find out Roman and Victor are bloodthirsty vampires, and now you're telling me there's more?"

He nods, still looking very serious. "They're not the only vampires in Lithia."

"What?"

He opens his mouth, and I watch in horror as two fangs form, stalactite-like, and extend. My heart feels as though it's stopped, and I back up, dead-ending into a tree.

"Kat, relax. It's okay," he says.

His words remind me of Victor's, just before he came in for the kill—*Don't worry. It won't hurt*—and without a moment's hesitation, I turn and start to run.

But I don't know where I'm going. Unlike last night, there's no trail, and I have no idea which way to turn. My legs are stiff and sore from yesterday, and my muscles are screaming in agony.

Then he is in front of me.

"Kat, it's not what you think," he says. I see his fangs, gleaming in the white mist.

I turn and run in the other direction. Again, he cuts me off.

This time, he's faster than I am. He reaches out and takes me by the arms. I hear the sound of my voice ripping through my throat, my scream echoing among the redwoods, and then everything goes black.

# Nineteen

I wake up, blinking the sun out of my eyes. As I adjust to the bright light, I see Alex on my right, kneeling over me, holding my arm firmly. My heart ramps up again, and I try to pull away from him.

"Easy, easy," he says.

"What happened?"

"You fainted."

"Where am I?" I'm struggling to take my arm back, to get away.

"You're safe, Kat. I won't hurt you. I would never hurt you."

"But—you're a vampire." I look at him closely, trying to see his fangs. But they've retracted, and he looks like Alex again, regular old Alex. Did I dream it all up?

Then he confirms, "Yes, I'm a vampire. But I'm not like

Roman. You'll have to let me explain."

I don't want to hear his explanation, but he's holding me so firmly I can't escape. My only option is to let loose a scream that can be heard for miles and hope to catch the attention of some hikers or campers. So I open my mouth, take a deep breath—and that's when I look around me.

And I see that we're not on the ground.

We're in a tree. But this is not just any tree. I'm stretched out across a thick branch that's as wide as a park bench, and surrounding me are treetops in every direction. When I glance down, I see the tree trunk disappear into mist, and I feel as though I might faint again.

"It's okay, Kat," Alex says. "You're safe up here. I won't let you fall. I promise."

"How did I get up here?"

"I carried you."

"Carried me?"

"That's right."

"But how—" I stop, remembering his fangs. He brought me up here where I have no way to escape. Except to jump.

My body begins to tremble. "What are you going to do to me?"

"Nothing," he says. "I'm just going to talk to you, that's all."

"Why can't we talk on the ground?"

"Because you were running from me. Up here, you can't go anywhere. I need you to listen to me."

"I don't know about you, but I find it really hard to focus when I'm scared out of my mind."

"I told you, I won't let you fall. You need to know the truth about me, Kat. Then I'll take you back down and let you go, and you'll never have to see me again if you don't want to. I promise."

I take a few deep breaths and tell myself that if he'd wanted to hurt me, he would have already. But then again, I thought the same about Roman. Is there no one I can trust?

I can't even scoot away from Alex, as much as I want to. I'm too afraid of falling. I look around and feel as though I'm at the top of a mountain peak; in all directions, all I see are the tops of trees. I'm surprised to see that the tree we're in rises another twenty or thirty feet above.

"This is the tree," I say, remembering what he said just before he bared his fangs. "We're in the tallest tree in the world?"

Alex nods. He stands up and holds out his hand. I take it, not so much because I forgive or trust him but because I know that holding onto him is the only certain way I won't go flying off this branch.

"When I was born," he says, "this tree was only a hundred feet tall."

"Wow," I say. "I didn't know they grew that fast."

"They don't." He pauses, then continues, "This tree is more than two thousand years old."

"I don't—" I stop when I realize what he's talking about. "Oh. The vampire thing."

He nods again. "When I come up here, I don't feel quite so old."

He looks wistful, but also a little peaceful. Nothing like the way Victor and Roman had looked at me last night. Like they were ready to devour me.

"What did you mean when you said you're not like Roman?" I ask.

"I don't live on blood."

"What do you mean?" I ask. "I thought that was the only thing a vampire can eat."

"Not me. Not anymore."

"What do you live on, then?"

"You're standing on it."

I look down, then look back at him. "Trees?"

"The blood of trees."

"The blood of—" It takes me a second to figure out what he's talking about. But then Roman's voice shoots through my mind: *sapsucker*. "Sap. You drink sap."

"Yes, I live on sap."

"I didn't know vampires could do that."

"As I told you, we're adaptable."

"You eat only from plants?"

"Exactly." He smiles. "So you see why I could never hurt you."

"A vegan vampire," I say, amazed to hear these words coming from my own mouth. Amazed that such a thing exists. Mostly, I'm relieved. My instincts have been right, maybe not about Roman, but about Alex. I am safe with him.

"Yes, a vegan vampire," Alex says.

"I've heard about vegetarian vampires," I say, "the ones that eat animals, not humans."

"Anyone who eats an animal, human or vampire, is not a vegetarian," Alex says. "To be vegetarian is to spare all mammals, all birds, all fish. But then, you know that already."

"Are you the only one?"

"There are others, but only a few. We have to keep a low profile, which is why I've waited so long to tell you. Many— vampires like Roman—believe it's okay, even admirable, to kill a vegan vampire. We are lesser creatures in their eyes. And we threaten their existence."

"So this is why you and Roman hate each other."

Alex nods. "We don't see eye to eye, to say the least. We're in completely different worlds."

"So why hasn't he killed you yet?"

Alex shrugs. "As they say, keep friends close and your

enemies closer. I think Roman and his type keep us around in case there's ever a need for a scapegoat. In case they ever need someone to blame. I also think he's worried. He tells himself that he can kill me easily—but what if he can't? If he doesn't try, he'll never need to know that I'm stronger. He can just go on believing it."

"So are you stronger?"

"I am now," he says. "But I wasn't so strong then. To be honest, I was close to ending my own life before I discovered the trees. Every time I took the life of a human, I was consumed with guilt. I couldn't help doing it, of course—it's the way I was made, and the instinct to live is so powerful. I always thought I had no choice. But it began to wear on me, all that death. I couldn't help but think of those left behind, waiting, hopelessly waiting. And I began to wonder why my existence had to come at the expense of another. It was not just a matter of eating to live. I had removed human beings from the earth—people who were husbands and wives and parents and children—never to return. The weight of murder was growing too heavy on my shoulders. So I tried to limit myself to animals."

"Did that work?"

"The guilt didn't go away. Who's to say a fawn doesn't miss its mother, just because it's a deer and not a human? Blood is blood in the end."

"So what happened?"

"I starved myself, but that only made me weak. And in my weakest moments, my instinct returned, and I went back to my old ways again. So I was left with only one option."

"And?"

Alex's voice grows quiet. "I sought out the tallest tree I could find. Which meant, naturally, that I ended up here. I fashioned a sharp stake made of ash and shoved it into the ground, pointing up. Then I started climbing."

"Oh, Alex."

"I climbed to the top," Alex continues. "And I prepared to jump and leave this world for good. But when I was up here, I caught a scent of something, something fragrant. It was coming from the trunk. And I was hungry again, so hungry—so I sank my teeth into the bark, like you'd bite into an apple. And then I drank."

"What was it like?" I am still stunned, thinking of Alex's fangs. Thinking of him drinking sap from a tree. Thinking of how he would rather have died than hurt another living creature.

"At first, the sap made me ill. Or so I thought—it was so different. I felt very hazy, very strange. I leaned against the trunk of this tree, four hundred feet in the air, and felt myself swaying, dizzy. I fell asleep—or I thought I did. I was dreaming, or maybe hallucinating, but all I could see were images of the world covered in green, this beautiful mossy green. Just like what you see on all these trees." He shakes his head. "I thought I was dead. But then I recovered, and when I came to my senses, I realized I was stronger than before. That I actually felt better. So I took another drink. Then another. And I felt my strength returning."

"How did you know you would survive?"

"I didn't. That is, I didn't have any proof. Deep down, though, I knew. There is a life force all around us. In trees, plants, animals—anywhere in nature. I just tap into it."

"But doesn't this harm the trees?"

"It doesn't have to. This was the first tree I ever drank from, and look how strong it is. You remember Roman calling me a sapsucker, don't you?"

"Who could forget?"

"He didn't mean it as a compliment, but I actually take it as one. A sapsucker is a small bird that also lives off the trees. If you look closely at certain trees, you can see the tiny holes the sapsucker drills with its beak. What sapsuckers know—and what we know, too—is that if a tree dies, we lose a source of food. So the sapsucker feeds off of a number of different trees. We do the same thing. We have learned to take as little as necessary from a tree, and to drink from many trees, always alternating, the way a farmer alternates crops."

"Symbiosis," I say. "That's smart."

"Nature is smart," he says. "In nature, there's no such thing as overconsumption. No such thing as waste. Everything in nature takes what it needs and nothing more."

"So you don't kill the trees that feed you?"

"No, we don't. Fortunately, in Lithia, we are next to a million acres of forest, a virtual smorgasbord. For all my long life, I assumed that not having blood meant certain death, that no vampire could survive without it. But I did. Not only that—I thrived. Just as I thought my life was over, it actually began. Now I'm free of the guilt, of the cycle of death." He smiles. "And, if I do say so myself, this diet has done wonders for my skin. You've seen how pale Roman is."

"Why hasn't Roman converted?"

"Roman doesn't see any reason to change his ways. If anything, seeing me go through this transformation only gives him more reason to cling to his ways. I called him an old-school vampire once, and he nearly fought me to the death. He talks of tradition and instinct and fate, like we are all frozen in amber. But we're not. If humans can change their diets, why can't we?"

"Do you still crave blood?"

"I used to, for the first few years. Any new habit requires letting go of an old habit. But since that day up here, I've never killed another human or animal. I'm proud of that."

"Roman has killed people, hasn't he?"

"What do you think?"

I know the answer, but I don't want to believe it. I don't want to believe that someone I once liked so much could be responsible for the deaths of others. Probably a great many deaths, which I don't want to think about either.

"Wait," I say. "He could have killed me weeks ago. Why didn't he? When I first got here, no one knew who I was. Nobody even would have noticed."

"I can think of two reasons why he didn't," Alex says.

"What are they?"

"For one, you're a vegan."

"What does that have to do with it?"

"To a vampire, the blood of a human vegan is no different than that of a deer. The blood will keep you alive, sure, but it won't taste the same, and it won't offer the same energy. I think it's because you don't eat meat that Roman doesn't crave your blood as much as others. It wouldn't satisfy him."

I think back to that first date with Roman, at the steak-house. Roman had pushed me to eat steak; he wanted me to change. Was he setting me up for the kill?

"That's why you made me promise to stay vegan."

"Right," Alex says. "I'm pretty sure he'll leave you alone as long as you are."

"But what if he changes his mind?" I ask with a shudder. "Or what if he gets so hungry that he can't help it?"

"That brings me to the second reason."

"Which is?"

"Roman seems to like you right where you are," Alex says. "He doesn't want to kill you."

"But shouldn't it be the opposite? I mean, if he does like me so much, wouldn't he want me to become a vampire like him? Eternal life and all that?"

"There are no guarantees," Alex says. "You might become a vampire, but you might also simply die, depending on your body's reaction. There are some antidotes, too. Roman probably wasn't ready to take that risk."

"But he might. Someday."

"Not on my watch," Alex says.

My heart does a little flip-flop in my chest. "I shouldn't have gone running last night without you," I confess. "I wish I hadn't. I just—I wanted to see if I could find Stacey up there. On the trail. I know it sounds silly."

"Not at all," he says. "But I'm glad you understand now."

"I miss her."

"I do, too." Alex reaches out and pulls me close to him, and we sit down in the tree, letting our legs dangle from the branch. I swing my legs back and forth, feeling free, knowing that Alex won't let me fall.

"Do you always come here to eat?" I ask him.

"Not always," he says. "It's fun for Thanksgiving. A good

place for a feast."

I laugh, and he laughs, too. I look up at him, at his happy face, and before I know what I'm doing, I'm reaching up to kiss him. He kisses me back.

I turn to move a little closer, and then I feel myself slipping, slipping off the rough bark of this tree, hundreds of feet in the air.

Then Alex is lifting me, pulling me back up with a preternatural strength I'd never have imagined.

"I won't let you fall," he promises again.

I lean my body against his. "Can we stay here forever?" I ask.

"We can try," he says, a smile in his voice, "except we both have to be at work tomorrow."

I sigh. "I guess you're right."

"But we'll stay here for a while," he says. "I want you to see this place after dark. From here, the stars are so much closer, you won't believe it. You feel like you can reach out and grab them."

He wraps his arms around me, and I lean back to look up at the sky. It's still early, and I'm glad. It means I have hours and hours, alone up here in this tree with Alex, before he'll want to show me the stars.

# Twenty

When I open the store the next morning, I go in through the back, as usual. When I'm ready to open the front doors, who do I find waiting for me but Roman, standing outside on the sidewalk. I'm tempted to ignore him and leave the CLOSED sign up, but David will be in later, and I don't think he will approve.

Still, I do try to ignore him as I unlock the doors and flip the sign. Roman sticks a toe in the door, wedging it open.

"Katherine," he says, "can we talk?"

I step outside onto the sidewalk, looking up and down the street to make sure there are witnesses. There aren't a lot of people out and about, but two homeless men are seated on a bench down the street, watching us. That's something, at least.

"Go ahead, talk," I say, standing in front of the door. I'm not about to let him inside.

"Victor is gone. And he's not coming back."

"Is that it? That's all you have to say?"

"I'm sorry I wasn't honest with you. It's not exactly something you mention on a first date."

"I see. So when were you planning to tell me you're a blood-sucking vampire? After our second date? Third? After we got married?"

"Married?"

Oops. I shouldn't have said that. He's flashing that gorgeous smile of his. The smile I was first attracted to.

"You know what I mean," I say.

"I know," he says, his smile fading, erased by a serious, apologetic look. Roman the actor—he is even better than I thought.

"Katherine, all I can tell you is that I'm sorry. I deceived you, and that wasn't fair. But sometimes I lose track of where the truth ends and the lies begin. Living here, among humans—everything I do is a lie, a deception."

"Yes," I say. "You live and breathe your work. It's all an act."

"When I'm on stage, that's the easy part. It's when the lights go back on that I struggle so."

"I'm sorry for your *struggle*, Roman," I say, "but the fact remains that you are no more than a serial killer."

This time, even the actor in him can't cover up the look

on his face. It makes me feel sorry for him. Almost.

"There's just one thing I don't understand," I say. "The other night—why did you defend me?"

"Isn't it obvious? I'm falling in love with you."

"But how can you be any different from Victor?" I say. "You're both vampires. You need to eat as much as he does, right?"

"I do. But you do me a disservice when you compare me to Victor. I would never hurt you."

"If you don't want to hurt me, how do you find it okay to hurt anyone else? Why not stop killing people altogether?"

"You know I can't do that."

"Alex did that."

His eyes grow dark and angry, and I feel like ducking into the store and locking the door. But it wouldn't do any good. I know his strength too well. So I hold my ground.

"What has Alex told you?" Roman asks.

"Everything. He told me you could change, if you wanted to."

"Alex is a freak of nature. He's not one of us."

"Not anymore, he's not. He's better than you. More important, he's more like *me.*"

"Katherine, you have no idea what you are asking of me."

"I'm asking you to change."

"You're asking me to give up who I am."

"I'm asking you to let people have an opportunity to run on that trail without getting attacked."

He lets out a scornful laugh. "Do you really think that vampires are the only things in those hills you have to worry about?"

"I'm not worried about the bears."

"Bears are not what I'm referring to," he says.

"Then what?"

"Let us just agree that Lithia is filled with—shall we say—spirits."

I shake my head. "Whatever, Roman. The fact remains that you have the power to change. To start over. To manifest a better world."

"Alex has brainwashed you, I see," Roman says. "With all his new-age proclamations about the environment."

"No. That's all mine."

"Alex is no saint. If only you knew…" Roman's voice trails off, and he turns his back to me.

"Knew what?"

He turns back.

"Do you think this is easy, Katherine—my life? I live among humans and yet I am not human. I will never be human, no matter how hard I try, no matter how many trees I hug. I'm destined to be an outsider, to live in darkness. I will always live in darkness. And for you to judge me by the standards of *your* life is not fair. If you compare me to most of the other humans you know, to most of the carnivorous people in this world, there is not such a void. They eat meat; they eat blood. I drink blood."

"They don't kill people for their food."

"But they kill nonetheless. A mere technicality in the greater scheme. Katherine, I was born this way. I will always be this way."

"I disagree," I say. "I think you can change. And I—"

Just then I notice a man across the street—it's that man who was following me the other day. I shake my head, as if to clear my vision, to try to get a better look. I'd been followed so often lately—by Victor, by Roman—that I'd basically forgotten about this guy. Yet there he is, about to cross over to our side of the street.

Roman swivels his head around to follow my gaze. "What is it?" he asks.

"Nothing," I say, but in the brief second it takes me to glance at Roman, the man disappears. I take a few steps away from the door and look up and down the street. He seems to have vanished, and this leaves me with a deep, tangled knot in my stomach.

When I return my attention to Roman, he's holding out an envelope.

"What's this?"

"A ticket. Tonight is the last performance of the season. My last evening as Hamlet. I'd be honored if you would attend."

"Roman, I don't think—"

"Please come," he says. "I know you're upset. I know I am no longer the man you thought I was. The regrets are all mine. I was asking too much of you. But for tonight, for one last night, please come. You know you'll be safe in the theater, even if you don't trust me again yet."

"I will never trust you again."

He continues to hold out the envelope, so finally I take it. I'll give it away—a reward for our first customer of the day. Because there's no way I'm going to spend a whole evening watching Roman on a stage, playing one of his roles.

After I accept his envelope, I wait for Roman to wink at me, or to smile his dangerous smile, but he simply turns and walks away. There is a sorrow to his gait, to the slouch in his shoulders; despite myself, I feel bad. After hearing Alex's story, I know how hard it must be for Roman to try to change. And now he and I are fighting a battle that neither of us can win.

But Alex has given me hope—he is living proof that change is possible. And I have hope for Roman, too. I have to. If he can't change, if I can't help him change, that means that more people will die.

I can't live with any more death in my life.

I look down at the envelope in my hand and pull out the

ticket. It's a good seat, front-row center. Maybe I won't give it away to the first customer after all. Maybe I'll think about it and decide later. I can always give it to the last.

———∽∽∽———

With Cloudline only a week away, the store is getting busier, and we are swamped all afternoon. Almost everyone who walks in the door is a new face to me, runners I've never seen before, though many seem to know David well. Old running buddies, friends from California and Washington and Idaho. I can see the pain on David's face as they offer condolences. Even though Cloudline brings in all the good business, I can tell that David is anxious to put the whole thing behind him.

Stacey had finished in the top ten at Cloudline over the past few years, and she made it to number five last year. Soon after we met, she'd told me that she was aiming for the top spot this year, that she was ready to unseat the runner who'd won the women's division for the past three years. She seemed very determined.

When I finally have a free moment, right around closing, I log on to the Cloudline website and look at last year's winners. When I see the photo of the women's division winner, I wince. It's the rude woman who'd come in a couple of weeks ago. Erica Summers. I remember how she'd bragged about winning.

I decide right then that I want to win this race. In honor of Stacey, I will unseat Erica, as Stacey should have been able to do herself. The thought even makes me smile a little, thinking of how happy Stacey would be if she could see it. And who knows—maybe she will be able to see it, somehow.

David comes over to ring up a customer, and I glance at my watch. It's a few minutes to closing, and I reach for the theater ticket in my pocket, ready to give it to this last customer.

And then, all of a sudden, I change my mind. Maybe it's because I've been thinking of Stacey, but I realize more than ever that the killings have to end. And this means I need to see Roman. That I need to change his mind. I can't accomplish anything if I ignore him.

So I leave the ticket in my pocket and look over at David. He seems to be a little better every day. Getting back to work has been good for him. I want to tell him about everything that's happened. That I know who killed Stacey. That it wasn't a bear but a vampire.

I feel he deserves to know the truth, but then, who am I really trying to help? Getting it off my chest would help *me*, but will it help him? How will telling him about Victor make him feel any better? There will be no justice. It won't bring Stacey back. Even worse, he will know that Victor is still out there somewhere, and many more vampires, too, and that women—and men and children and animals alike—are living in danger every day. And that's if he even believes me.

No, I can't say anything. It's another secret that I need to keep to myself.

I head toward the front doors to turn the sign over to CLOSED when I see Alex on the other side of the glass, reaching for the door handle. I smile at him and step outside. He leans over to give me a kiss.

"Busy day?" he asks.

"You have no idea. I was worried we'd run out of shoes."

"Do you want to go grab a coffee or something, before our run?"

"Oh," I say, remembering Roman and the *Hamlet* ticket, which suddenly feels as though it's burning a hole in my pocket. "I—I don't think I'll be able to run tonight. My muscles are pretty raw, and David's going to need a lot of help cleaning up. Restocking the shelves. Stuff like that."

"Really?"

"I'm sorry." I hope my face isn't as red as it feels. "I know I shouldn't take too much time off. I hope I can still make it through Cloudline."

"It's just one night. You'll be fine." He studies me, a suspicious look on his face. "We'll run tomorrow then, okay?"

"Yes," I say. "Absolutely."

He takes my hand and squeezes it, and I squeeze back, hard, trying to convince him that everything is fine. Or maybe trying to convince myself.

———∿∿———

In the darkened theater, I no longer see Hamlet on that stage, as I did last time. Now, I see only Roman. A vampire playing an actor playing a role. And I find my heart going out to him, despite what he is, what he does. After all, I know what it's like to act, to pretend you're happy when you're not. To feel alone.

Every line he utters seems to take on new meaning—his words seem as though they're coming not from a play but from his life. He knows exactly where my seat is, and he looks at me directly several times during the performance, just as he'd done before. Only then, I thought I imagined it. Now, I know.

> *But that the dread of something after death,*
> *The undiscover'd country from whose bourn*
> *No traveller returns, puzzles the will*
> *And makes us rather bear those ills we have*
> *Than fly to others that we know not of?*
> *Thus conscience does make cowards of us all...*

Death. The undiscover'd country. Not for Roman. He has not only gone there and discovered it, but he remains there. And he always will. I try to imagine what that must be like, to be trapped in a place you can never escape. I have always hated being on the run, but it's only now that I realize that maybe I am lucky. I've always thought of my situation as a curse, but maybe it's actually a gift to be able to leave a place and never look back. To outrun my mistakes. Roman can't do that.

But what he can do is change. He can't change what he's done in the past, any more than I can—but he can change his future. And this will be a sort of escape for him, or at least it's as close to an escape as he can get. From the guilt. From a future of more pain. From a life that never felt like his own.

I look up at the stage, and I watch Roman die once again, laid out before me, wounded by a poisoned sword. I watch him utter out his last line—*The rest is silence*—before going still.

I wait by the back door of the theater, and after half an hour, the actors begin to exit; to sign autographs; to make their way home, to dinner, to bars. I stand back in the shadows and watch as Roman emerges. He patiently signs every program and a few T-shirts, mostly for awed young girls on school trips. He graciously stands next to them and smiles. I can tell that this takes almost as much effort as the role of Hamlet.

But when I step forward and he sees me, he smiles— this time a full smile, a real smile. "Katherine. Thank you for coming."

"I thought I'd surprise you."

"Would you like to go for a walk?" he asks, extending a hand.

I pause and look at his face, his eyes. He looks tired, but I don't even know if that's possible. Do vampires get tired? Or maybe he's just weary. That's a different kind of tired but one that shows on your face just the same.

I'm not sure I should, but I take his hand. We walk down a long flight of stairs to the entrance of Manzanita Park. The same park where I almost spent my first night in Lithia. I was so frightened then, so lost. Now, I'm no longer afraid of the park, though I probably should be afraid of my walking companion.

"I would like to take you on another date," Roman says. "A vegetarian restaurant."

"Really?" I watch his nose wrinkle even as he nods yes. "You would do that for me?"

"Well, I might have to eat beforehand."

He clearly means this as a joke, but when he says *eat*, all I can see are images of him and Victor in the woods. Victor leaning over me. Just as he'd leaned over Stacey.

I drop his hand and stop walking. "Roman, this isn't going to work. I don't know what I'm doing here with you. I—"

He holds up a hand to silence me. "Someone is watching us," he whispers.

"Where?" I'm worried that it's Alex, that he knows I cancelled our run to spend the evening with Roman. I search the darkness but I can't see anything.

Roman, looking to our left, does see something, and he calls out, "I know you're there. Show yourself."

I follow Roman's eyes, and all of a sudden I can make out the outline of a man. He's coming toward us, and as he gets closer, I recognize him. The medium build, the balding head. The khakis. He is looking right at me.

"Who are you?" Roman asks.

"That's not important. I'm not looking for you."

"If you are here for her, that is my concern," Roman says.

"I've been hired to find your friend here. Ms. Katherine Healy."

"You've got the wrong Katherine," Roman says. "This is Katherine Jones."

"Is it now?" The creepy man smiles. "I know someone who thinks differently."

I feel a sharp stab of panic in my chest. "Leave us alone," I say.

"I can't do that."

"She asked to you leave." Roman steps toward the man, and he backs up. I have to admit that I'm grateful to have a vampire on my side at a time like this.

"Easy now." The man holds out his hand, like he's calming an agitated dog, then he pulls his arm back to reveal a handgun holstered to his waist. "I don't want any trouble. I just want a few minutes alone with Katherine."

"That is not going to happen."

"You don't get to make the decisions, pal," the man says.

In a blink, Roman grabs the man by his neck with one hand and strips away his gun with the other. The man's legs are off the ground, flailing; Roman is holding him in midair. I can hear the man struggling to breathe. I feel as though I've stopped breathing myself.

"Roman, stop," I say. I want this man gone, but not this way.

Roman looks at me. "Run straight home, fast. Go to David's and lock the doors."

"But—"

"Now," he says.

And I have no choice but to obey.

# Twenty-one

I run home, but not to David's. He is still up—all the lights are on—but first I go to the cottage, where I pack my bag. Again.

This time, I have to leave. For good. But this time, I will say goodbye. First to David, then to Alex.

It's for the best. After all, David isn't even sure whether he himself will stay, without Stacey. And if he sells the store, I'm out of a job.

Besides, I have no choice. That man knows my name. My real name. I wonder if he is a cop. Or a detective. Most of all, I wonder how he found me.

Because I haven't gone far enough. That's how.

How far do I have to run before I can be free?

Maybe, like Roman, I'll never be free. Maybe I'm stuck, just like he is. In this moment, I can understand his gloom, his unwillingness to change. Why try to make things better when you're going to end up right back where you started anyway?

I wonder what Roman is doing, or has already done, to that man. I'm afraid to know. But I'm even more afraid of him coming after me.

I hear a tap on my door and freeze where I am. Maybe I should've gone directly to David's after all.

I don't answer, and I hear another knock, then David's voice.

With relief, I open the door. "You're up late," David says.

I glance behind me, hoping he doesn't see my backpack on the bed, half packed. I haven't figured out what I'm going to tell him. "Um, yeah. I'm just cleaning up a little."

"Well, I don't want to bother you," he said, "but I wanted to give you something." He hands me a shoe box. "They just came in."

I crack open the lid to see a new pair of Brooks trail shoes, much like the pair I'm wearing—but these are built for trail running, with firmer soles and waterproof covering.

"Wow," I say. "These are beautiful. They're going to be popular, with Cloudline coming up."

He gives me a strange look. "I should've been more clear," he says. "This pair is for you."

I don't know what to say. "I can't accept these, David. They're too—too good. And I already have shoes."

"Yours are fine running shoes, but you've worn them down, and I can't even tell what the original color was. These are trail shoes, the very best. And if you're going to win Cloud-line, you need the best shoes."

It's as if he knows, somehow, about my silent vow to win the race. I never told him.

"I love them," I say. He is making it impossible for me to say no. To these shoes, and to Lithia. "But I've already accepted so much from you, and I've done nothing in return."

"You've kept the store running," David says. "You've helped me through some of the worst days of my life. I couldn't have done it without you."

"But—" I choke up and can hardly talk. "But it's only because of me that—"

I start to cry, and David puts his arms around me.

"It was my fault," I say. "I left her behind. I'm so sorry."

"You are not responsible for Stacey," he says. "You never were. And I should never have asked you to look after her—it was wrong. It was too much to ask of anyone."

He pulls away so he can look at my face, which I know is red and tear-streaked. "I knew Stacey very well," he says. "She and I had our differences, but part of what drove me crazy was also what I loved the most. Like her stubbornness. She was running that trail long before you came along, and she would've been doing it even if you'd never shown up in Lithia.

And she'd never let anyone tell her not to. There is nothing anyone could have done. It was her time."

David gets me a tissue. As he does, he sees my backpack on the bed.

"Kat," he says, "what's going on?"

I begin to cry again. "Nothing," I say.

"It looks like you're going somewhere. Are you?"

"I've been thinking about it."

"Why?"

I look at him, and he looks so sad, like he doesn't want me to go.

"Kat?" he says. "What is it?"

I decide to tell him. "When I came here," I say, "I was running away from something. From someone. And now I don't know what to do."

"What was it?"

"I—I can't say."

He studies my face. "Are you in any danger?"

I think of Roman. Of his hands around that guy's neck. "No, I don't think so. Not right now, anyway."

"But you were, is that it?"

"Yes," I say. "I was."

David comes over and lifts my chin to look me in the eye. "Kat, you're safe here. I hope you know that. Come over and stay in the guest room tonight if you'd like."

"Okay." I blow my nose with the tissue he gave me. "Thank you."

"I want you to know that I'm keeping the store," he says. "I decided this afternoon. And there's a full-time job there for you if you want it."

"Really?"

"It doesn't mean you have to stay. But I'd like you to."

"I would, too. But I don't know if I can."

"How about this?" he says. "Run Cloudline. Finish the race, then decide. Will you do that?"

"Okay."

"Good," he says. "Now, I want you to take these shoes. And I want you have this, too." David reaches into the pocket of his jacket and hands me Stacey's custom running cap. The bright orange one with the "S" on the back.

"Oh, I can't," I say.

"Stacey would want you to have it," he says.

I hesitate. "Are you sure?"

"Positive," he says. "It doesn't fit me. And when I bought it, I knew that the woman wearing it would be the first one to cross the finish line. And now, that's going to be you."

—∿∿—

The next day after work, I lace up my shoes and jog away

from the store. I am supposed to meet Alex at the co-op for a run—a short workout before the race tomorrow. But instead of heading for the co-op, I find myself circling around it. I'm still trying to decide what to do, and I haven't had any time alone to think.

I snake back and forth on Lithia's streets for a while, but it's not the same as being on the trail. I have to wait for lights, dodge pedestrians, watch for cars. I can't think here either. I want to head for the trails, where I can be alone, at peace—but I've promised Alex I wouldn't. And this is one promise I plan to keep.

I hear a voice shout my name, and when I glance over my shoulder, I see a figure in the shadows of the streetlights running toward me, quickly. I can't see who it is, so automatically I accelerate, heading for Main Street, for heavy traffic and crowds of people.

I hear the footsteps getting closer. There's a gas station ahead, brightly lit with people and cars, and I run toward it. The footsteps are right behind me now, but oddly, I don't hear the sound that should accompany it—the sound of someone out of breath. As soon as I'm under the bright lights of the station, I stop and turn.

It's Roman.

I breathe, leaning down and resting my hands on my knees.

"Why are you running from me?" he asks.

"Because you were chasing me. I thought you were that guy. From yesterday."

"You no longer have to concern yourself with him," Roman says.

Roman's wearing running gear, head to toe, and I remember that he, too, is taking one last run before Cloudline. His skintight tank top exposes his broad shoulders; the black tights display sculpted legs.

I look at him. "What does that mean, I don't have to be concerned about him?"

"You think I hurt him."

"I worry you did more than hurt him."

"I didn't."

"How can I believe you?"

"You'll have to take my word for it. I could have killed him, very easily, and nobody would have been the wiser. Believe me, I was tempted."

"How am I supposed to believe you didn't?" I say. "It's what you do, isn't it?"

"Do you think this is easy for me?" Roman asks, and I hear in his voice the same anguish I heard when he was on stage, playing Hamlet. Roman's never been emotional, except on stage, and it takes me by surprise. "I eat very seldom, Katherine, and I usually travel far away from here when I do."

"You think that makes it better?"

"No, but it makes it easier. You don't understand. When we get hungry, we don't realize what we do. It's as if we go into a trance. What you think is barbaric—for us, it's normal."

"But you're living in a world where it's not normal."

"Katherine, I did not harm that man last night. I escorted him to his car, and I watched him drive out of town. I'll admit I made sure he would not come back, yes. But I didn't hurt him."

I look at him doubtfully.

"You are in a strange position to be so judgmental."

"What are you talking about?"

Roman holds up small notebook. "I lifted this from the man's coat. You may be interested in its contents, Ms. Healy."

I grab for it, and he holds it out of my reach. "We all have our secrets, Katherine. We all live with mistakes."

"Give me that," I demand, and he lowers his arm.

I take the notebook and open it, holding it up to the light. Inside is a minute-by-minute breakdown of my life over the past week. Nothing more.

"What's this for?" I ask. "Who was he?"

"A private investigator. From Texas. Do you know anyone in Texas who might want you followed?"

"No," I say, but I can tell Roman is unconvinced. As unconvinced as I am that he let that man go.

I feel the night close in on me. But I'm not telling him

anything. I can't.

"Are you sure you don't have something to tell me?" Roman asks. "He was being paid a tidy sum to follow your every move. That usually doesn't happen to people who have nothing to hide."

"Did he say who hired him?"

"Why are you using a different name?" Roman counters.

"I asked you first."

"Katherine, I know what it's like to have secrets," Roman says. "And I'm quite certain that I can handle yours, whatever they are."

"Have you told me all of *your* secrets, Roman?" I'm getting defensive. He's the vampire, after all; why is he interrogating me? Besides, I'm not prepared to talk about my life.

"Some secrets are too painful to share," Roman says quietly.

"Then stop asking me to share mine."

Roman sighs. "I was not completely forthright about this investigator."

"So you did kill him."

"No, I did not. Truly," he says. "But he told me who hired him."

I feel an awful pressure, like strong hands squeezing my heart, making it hard to breathe. "Who?"

"Your father."

The grip tightens. "That's impossible."

"That's what he said."

"Then he lied to you," I say. "Or you're lying to me."

"I'm not lying."

"Then that investigator lied to you."

"What makes you so certain?"

"My father is dead," I say.

Roman looks at me, puzzled. "This man seems to think otherwise. One of you clearly has the wrong information."

"He's dead," I repeat.

"And you are sure about that?"

"I'm positive," I say. "I'm the one who killed him."

# Twenty-two

The night before a race is often a sleepless one. At least, it's always been that way for me. And most of the girls I ran with in high school also got stressed the night before a competition. Our coach would tell us that it doesn't matter if you don't sleep well the night before a race—as long as you get a good night's sleep *two* nights before a race. This helped relax us, and it changed our focus, so on the night before our races we all slept like babies. He'd tricked our restless minds, and it worked.

I wish I could do that now—find a way to take my mind off everything, or at least to divert my thoughts somewhere, anywhere. I've been tossing and turning all night, not with thoughts of the race but of everything else. I wish the race itself were enough to distract me. I welcome it now more than ever—a chance to get out on the trails, to put my body up to a task so challenging that during those hours I'll be able to focus on nothing else.

But eventually the race will be over, and whatever happens during the race won't change what I have to face after I cross the finish line. Because then, for me, the real race will just be beginning.

I look over at my alarm clock. Still a half an hour to go. At this point, sleeping will only make me groggy, so I sit up and turn it off.

The sun hasn't risen above the hills yet, and in the darkness of my cottage, I stand and stretch. I eat an energy bar and drink some water. I have two hours before the race starts.

I sit down, continuing with a few gentle stretches, letting my body warm up. I think of Stacey. How much I want to win this for her. I'm still so grateful to her for taking me in. For giving me a job. For never asking the questions I've been so afraid of. No one ever has, until last night. Until Roman.

And again I'm realizing that he and I are not so different after all. Maybe this is what I'm afraid of—that I've been drawn to him because we are both cut from the same murderous cloth. Our reasons may be different, but in the end, am I any better than he is?

Roman's reaction last night was odd. When I told him I killed my father, he nodded sadly. He touched my face, briefly, and he said, *Such secrets can seem impossible to bear, can't they,*

*Katherine?* That was all he said. And I told him nothing more. If nothing else, Roman understands the nature of secrets. How they can't be revealed too soon. And sometimes not at all.

I wanted to cancel my scheduled jog with Alex, but I knew it was too important to get in that last run. I was silent the entire time, wondering whether I could tell him what Roman now knows. Whether he would understand. He asked me what was wrong, but I ended up telling him I was nervous about the race. I couldn't take the risk that he will hate me for what I've done.

I stand up and jog in place for a few moments, then put on a layer of sweats over my running shorts and top. It's almost time to go.

The last time I competed was in high school, my junior year. It was June, during the state championships for cross country. I had yet to win a race, but I knew I could win this one. I knew I was ready. The week before, I'd won a training race against the seniors, though it was totally by accident. I had misheard Coach Penn, and I thought we were running a 10K instead of a 15K. So I set off at a 10K pace, and the girls shouted at me as I passed them. *What are you doing? Slow down!* But I didn't understand—in fact, I was surprised at how slow they were going. Soon I had left them far behind. We were on a trail, doing five-kilometer laps, and as I came up on the end of lap two, I saw coach Penn there with his trusty wristwatch. I picked up my pace, ready for my big finish—but when I crossed the mark I heard him yell out, *Great job, Katie! Only one more to go!*

I thought I'd heard him wrong, but when I stopped and looked back at him, he stared back as if to say, *Well, what are you waiting for?* So I started running again, too embarrassed to confess that I had made a mistake. So I had to do one more lap at this breakneck pace. Those were the longest three miles of my life. My arms grew heavy, and my lungs heaved for oxygen, but I refused to stop. I began slowing down, and I could sense the pack catching up with me. I pictured the grins on their faces, their smug expressions. I knew they were waiting for me to crash. *She started out too fast,* they would say. *We knew she'd never make it.*

I couldn't let them have the satisfaction. So I hobbled on. And when I neared the end of that final lap, I saw Coach Penn and knew I was going to win. With a hundred yards to go, knowing I could do it gave me the energy to pick up the pace. I finished strong, setting a personal best.

The coach was impressed. *If this were a race, you'd have set a course record,* he said.

As I cooled down, pacing through a patch of grass, I watched the rest of the team come in. They no longer looked at me dismissively, as they'd done all year. I had earned their respect. And I felt something I had never felt before. I felt important.

I won the state title that year, and I started getting emails and calls from recruiters. I could hardly believe it: College— freedom—was within my grasp.

Until the morning that my dad, coming home drunk at seven o'clock after being out all night, drove over my left foot.

I'd been on the sidewalk, waiting for the bus, when he called me over to the car. He said he had to ask me something, but I never found out what it was. I was standing next to the driver's-side window when suddenly the car pitched back- ward, rolling over my foot. He'd put it into reverse instead of park, and he was still so drunk that he stepped on the gas with- out even realizing it.

The pain was excruciating, but he was no help. He couldn't even drive me to the hospital, so I had to call a cab and wait. I sat on the curb, shaking and sick with pain, for twenty minutes before crawling into the backseat of the taxi.

And so my senior year was over before it began. I wouldn't run again for months, and the recruiters moved on. My dad never apologized. Up to the day I ended his life, I'm not sure he remembered doing it. I'd always been too afraid of his anger to remind him, even to ask.

Even if he had remembered, he wouldn't have admitted to doing it. He never thought he did anything wrong. I was the reason he was miserable in life. And before me, it was my mother. Years before, Mom and I used to have each other, but after she died, I was alone, his anger and bitterness directed squarely at me.

He didn't hit me often in those last years—I learned how to stay away. But that didn't make it much easier—what I wanted most was something I could never get from him. My mother had been the only one who made me feel loved.

I still miss her. And I know that one of the reasons I was so happy to have met Stacey was that she was about my mother's age, early thirties, when she died. Not that Stacey could have taken my mom's place, but whenever I was with her I had that same feeling of being looked after, being taken care of.

When I win this race, it will be for both of them. I try to picture them together, somewhere, watching me run. Cheering me on.

I pick up Stacey's cap and put it on. It fits me perfectly.

---

There are almost two hundred runners near the starting line, shedding their warm-up suits, stripping down to tank tops and shorts, hopping from foot to foot as they try to stay warm. I look up to see where the race is headed, but the trail is hidden in clouds. The fog drips down the hills like dry ice.

I stretch my legs and look around. I recognize a few faces

from town, and I can tell they recognize me. I don't see either Roman or Alex. A man in a Cloudline T-shirt and a Race Official badge stands on a platform and blows the whistle around his neck. Everyone quiets down.

"Hey, folks, listen up! We got the latest weather report from the top of the mountain, and it's *ugly*."

The crowd erupts in cheers.

"Be advised that you will encounter freezing rain, heavy fog, and, at four-thousand feet, snow. Hypothermia is a real danger, as are broken limbs and frozen fingers. The race will go on, but I am urging anyone who is not one-hundred percent sure of themselves to take this year off. Please."

The crowd is quiet as his words sink in, and I can see people taking a gut check.

"There is no shame in that," he continues. "I've run this race a dozen times, and even I would consider taking a pass this year. It's that nasty."

I watch the runners look at one another, as if waiting for someone else to make the first move. Then an older guy in a green tank top turns and walks away. And it's as if he has given permission to a dozen others, who also begin walking back to their cars. I look down at my new trail runners, and I shudder at the thought of ruining them on the climb. Or of falling, breaking something, getting frostbite. But there is no way I'm skipping this race.

I touch the "S" on my cap. I know I am meant to be here, to be running now. Especially when I look ahead and see Erica, wearing her number 1, heading through the crowd toward the front. I know Stacey wouldn't let a little snow stop her.

Then I see Roman walking toward me. He seems the same as always, undaunted by what I told him last night. He looks at my running cap. "It looks as though you're running for Stacey."

I nod.

"Good luck, Katherine," he says.

"Good luck to you, too." I watch him follow Erica to the front.

I hear someone call my name, and I look behind me to see Alex jogging over. He's wearing the number 11. I'm wearing number 117, so I am stuck in the back.

"What are you doing all the way back here?" I ask.

"I like to hang back in the pack. Maybe it's an underdog thing." He grins. "You mind if we start together?"

"Fine with me," I say. "Though it won't be long before I leave you in the dust."

He laughs. "Actually, I hope you do."

"Any last-minute pearls of wisdom?"

"Pace yourself," he says. "The race doesn't begin until you reach the boulders."

"The boulders?"

"You'll know them when you see them," Alex says. "From there to the finish line, anything can happen."

The man on the podium is now holding up an air horn. "Folks, we are thirty seconds from the start."

"Go get 'em," Alex says.

"See you at the top," I say.

My stomach is all nerves, my legs and arms numb from the cold. I'm ready to go. I look up the mountain and see trees extending into fog, then thick dark clouds, then nothing. It's probably better that I can't see the top of the mountain; it feels closer this way.

The horn blares. I'm shuffling as runners push toward the line, then I'm walking, then jogging, then running.

# Twenty-three

So much about running is about time. In a competition, you're racing time as much as you're racing the other runners. But what I have found is that you often have to lose track of time in order to improve your time. That is, you have to silence the clock in your head and let yourself go.

This is one reason I no longer wear a watch. And I no longer need to: Right now, as I head up into the mountains, there is a small plastic device, about the size of a tube of lip balm, fitted to my shoe, woven through my shoelaces. This device sent a signal out when I crossed the starting line, and it will send out another when I cross the finish line. So I don't have to worry about keeping track of my race time, even though I began at the rear of the pack.

The trouble is, during a race, it is nearly impossible to avoid thinking about time. There is usually somebody standing at each mile marker shouting out splits. And there are the incessant, recurring beeps from the wristwatches of other runners, helping them keep pace, which in turn reminds me of mine.

Back in the days when I ran regular races, I learned to separate myself from the other runners; I learned how to rediscover silence, even if it was only in my own head, and this is what I am trying to do now as I reach mile four. We have not yet entered the clouds hovering just above, but the trail is already blurred with mist. There are two men about twenty yards ahead of me and a few others close behind me. It's hard to run side by side on this trail because it is so narrow. As I pass other runners, I often have to sprint around them to avoid slipping off the trail's edge, where the forest envelops us like thousands of wooden arms.

I've already lost time trying to pass two men who were chatting with each other. See, there I am, thinking about time again—it's more difficult to put it out of my head than I remembered. So I remind myself that if I'm going to win this race, it will be by coming from behind. That it's still early. That it's okay to be where I'm at right now, far back. I know that Erica is at the front with a small group of elite female runners, and that they are pushing each other plenty hard. But, as Alex told me last week, the mountain pushes you hard enough as it is. You don't need anyone else.

Before long, we are in the clouds, and though I hear the sounds of breathing and footsteps ahead of me, behind me, and on the trails below and above me, I rejoice in the visual silence, the sense that it is just me and the mountain right here, right now. It's only an illusion of solitude, I know, but it relaxes me.

Yet it also, I realize, frees my mind to wander. And this isn't such a good thing.

Despite my best efforts, I find myself thinking back to that night in Houston. Maybe it's because I've spent all these months trying *not* to think about it that the memories come rushing back, as steadily as the wind in the trees above me.

And then there's the private investigator and what he told Roman. That he'd been hired by my father. Which is impossible.

Unless my father had lived. Could it be?

I replay that last night in my head. My father drunk, as usual. Waving around the gun that he kept in his bedroom, which was not usual. Even he knew better not to touch that gun when he was drunk. He wasn't a smart man, but he was smart enough to know he couldn't be trusted around it in that condition.

So I took it from him, snatched it out of his limp hand when he was reaching for another beer. He yelled and spun around, taking a swing at me. He stumbled as I ducked out of his way. And then I pointed his gun at him.

I have to admit, I was tempted to pull the trigger right then. To be free of him forever. I'd stayed with him all that time only because there were so few places to go. I didn't want to be on the street. I wanted to go to college, to get away—and I thought the only way to do that would be to stick it out with my dad. To put up with it all because it was a free place to stay. And because it wouldn't be for long.

But sometimes even a short time can be too long.

I used to wonder what my mother saw in him. He was never nice to me, or to her, at least not that I can remember. I don't know if he ever loved us; he sure never said so. Every once in a while—one of the rare times when his gambling paid off instead of driving him deeper into debt, or when he was between his first and third beer—in these brief moments, sometimes, I could see that he was once a happy man. That there might've been a tiny chance he could be happy again one day, if he ever wanted to be. But I guess he didn't see that for himself, and he never did anything differently, except to drink more, create more debt, and blame everyone but himself for the problems he caused.

When I held that gun on him, I felt in control for the first time in my life. I told him to sit down, and he did. It was the first time he'd ever done anything I'd asked.

But I'm not the violent type, and he knew it. And he knew

I didn't even know how to use a gun. I never went near it, and I wasn't even sure if this was his only one. So when he began to tease me, to dare me to shoot, I found my finger on the trigger; I found myself coming close. But still I couldn't do it.

When he rushed at me, it was a shock—partly because I thought he knew, even as I pointed the gun at him, that I wouldn't actually shoot; and partly because he was so drunk I didn't think he was capable of moving that fast. But he leapt at me, knocked me down, and then his hand was on the gun, trying to take it from me. I heard a firecracker in the alley next door, and he went limp on the floor next to me.

That's when I knew it wasn't a firecracker. That the gun had gone off.

He was lying facedown on the floor, not moving.

I had shot him. Or he had shot himself—I didn't even know, with both of our hands on the gun at the same time. I didn't even know what had happened until he collapsed. But in that instant I remembered that a small part of me had been tempted to do it. And then it didn't really matter whether it was me who pulled the trigger or not—just the knowledge that I'd wanted to made it feel like first-degree homicide.

I saw my life slipping away—for good this time, not in the tiny little ways it had been slipping all those years before— and I knew that I couldn't take the chance of hoping someone would understand that it was an accident. That it was self-defense. That he might've even done it himself. It felt like the final act of someone who'd lived in fear for her whole nineteen years.

So I dropped the gun and ran. And I've been running ever since.

Along the way, I checked the papers, the police reports. Nothing. But I didn't know what this meant. We had no family. He had few friends. He was always in trouble, and just one more drunken murder in Texas wasn't likely to be big news outside the neighborhood. So I kept running. I held my breath, and finally, around the time I arrived in Lithia, I was feeling as though I might finally be free.

But you're never free from your past. Never truly free.

Could he really be alive?

I'm not sure what to wish for. I want the reassurance that I didn't kill him, that he is okay. But on the other hand, if he is alive, if by some dark miracle he did survive, he'll make my life worse than it ever was. That private investigator is only a sign of what's to come, none of it good. I've seen only two things motivate my father—money and revenge. And nothing would motivate him more than getting back at the person who shot him in the chest and left him to die.

A sharp left on the trail brings me back into the race; we're heading up a steep grade. The half-dozen runners in front of me downshift into slow motion, leaning into the hill, gasping for breath.

I pass them quickly, my body fueled entirely by the fear and anger pumping through my system. The fear of my dad catching up with me. The anger, for everything, that I've held onto for too long.

Maybe he is waiting for me at the top of the mountain, with a sheriff in tow. And now I'm thinking, So what? Now, as the trail gets steeper, my mind has no more room for worry; it takes all my energy to keep my legs moving, to keep my breathing steady. Let them take me to prison in shackles. At least I will make it to the top.

The mist has thickened into a soup-like mix that prevents me from seeing more than fifty yards in any direction. I am alone again, and I must be making good progress. I've left several slowing runners behind, and I feel as though I'm in the nether land between the large, main pack of runners and the small lead pack. And though I have no idea how close I am to that lead pack, I'm happy to be ahead of the rest.

And then, suddenly, I am falling.

It was a tree root, I think, that tripped me—I hadn't been paying close enough attention—and I feel myself tumbling, scraping my way down rocks and bushes, very much the way I'd plummeted down the mountain trying to escape Victor and Roman. It seems as though I'll fall forever—until I stop at last, when my head slams against a tree.

The blow is fierce, and it may even have knocked me out for a moment. When I open my eyes, I blink into the white nothingness all around me, looking up at the tree that stopped my fall. I'm bleeding from a large gash below my left knee. I can see hardly anything else, I'm so fogged in. I know which was is up, thanks to the steepness of the mountain slope I'm sprawled on, but I can't see the trail. I can't see or hear any other runners.

That's it. The race is over. I'm done.

I begin to get to my feet, slowly. I'm thinking maybe I'll head down the mountain through the woods. I can't use the trail because it's filled with runners, and there's no point in trying to get back into the race. I've already lost precious minutes, and I don't know how many more I'll lose just trying to find my way back.

Then I see movement in the fog above me—a figure, or, rather, the shadow of a figure. I peer at it through the mist, thinking it's a runner, that maybe I am closer to the trail than I think. But there is no trail where this figure is.

A shiver goes through me as I remember something Roman said to me: *Lithia is filled with—shall we say—spirits.*

And just like that, the figure rushes toward me, and as I close my eyes, I feel it whoosh past, and then it's gone.

But it's enough to get me running again.

With a fresh jolt of adrenaline coursing through me, I

suddenly feel as though I can get back in the race. Maybe not finish anywhere close to the top, with my aching head and my bleeding leg, but enough to get back in and finish it at least. To be able to say I've run Cloudline.

But even as I run back uphill, I'm not getting to the trail. It seems to have disappeared. How far off the path did I fall?

I hear a sound behind me and I glance over my shoulder. I see it again—a giant, shadowy figure, growing larger, gaining on me. The strange thing is that it's completely silent. Even Roman and Victor had made noise, had announced their presence in the forest.

Now I'm sprinting, not knowing where I'm going, glancing behind me and taking my cue from this ghostly being, steady and looming behind me, forcing me to move faster and faster, to turn this way and that, hardly aware of the energy I'm exerting, running as if I've got the finish line in sight.

And then the ground shifts and I'm on the trail again, still sprinting all out, running like a madwoman.

I glance behind me. Nothing is there. Nothing but the distant bobbing shapes of a couple of runners pushing their way up the mountain.

My breath is coming smoothly and steadily, as though I've been keeping a steady pace all along. As if I haven't just been running for my life. I notice that my head no longer aches, and that's when I glance down at my injured leg.

There's no blood. Only a few splatters of mud from the trail.

I want to believe this was just part of my mind wandering, but I know better. I remember the night Alex and I sat in his favorite tree, waiting for the stars to come out. He told me that we're never alone in the forest—but he wasn't referring to the animals. He said, *There are beings not known to most humans. Who have remained hidden by choice.*

*You mean like ghosts?* I asked him.

*Call them that if you'd like. Maybe you'll meet one someday. They will make themselves known to people who are in tune with nature. When the time is right.*

*Are they scary?* I asked. *Do they hurt people?*

At this he laughed. *Of course not,* he said. *They're there to take care of you. If you need them. They exist to take care of the planet—but they know that this planet can't survive unless the humans take care of it, too. So sometimes, they need to take care of all of you.*

Now I'm wondering if I encountered one of these beings. Was this what had chased me back to the trail?

I've lost all track of time, of the miles. I am still passing people, but I don't know whether these are the runners I've already passed. Yet I feel fine, and I keep running.

Up ahead, I see what looks like a gateway cut out of stone. As I get closer, I see that the gateway is actually several huge rocks, taller than trucks, lining each side of the path as if they were placed there by giants.

The boulders.

Just like Alex said. This is where the race begins.

I pick up my pace, slowly at first but then with more confidence, amazed that I still have the energy to keep going. The hill is so steep at times that I can almost reach out and touch the ground in front of me, like shaking someone's hand.

I hear voices ahead and then I see two women holding cups of water. The last water station.

"One mile to go," the first woman says.

I can't believe it. I'm almost there.

"You're only three back!" the other woman says.

I must have heard her wrong, but as she shoves the water into my hand, I realize I heard correctly.

I slow a bit as I drink the water, splashing it all over my face and shirt. Only three back. Erica and another woman—and me.

The sky seems to brighten, as if it's dawn, and I look up and glimpse a patch of blue sky above. Alex had told me that by the end of the race, we might emerge above the clouds. Sure enough, the fog ahead is thinning out, and I see a woman ahead, tall and lean, wearing shorts with slits up to her waist. She's moving slowly past a tall bank of rocks, and I quickly pass her by. Past the rock pile there's more blue sky and only a handful of men ahead, not so much running the trail as climbing it.

I still have half a mile to go. Half a mile to catch Erica, and I don't even see her. I push myself further.

Straining my eyes against the bright light, I see Erica a hundred yards ahead of me on the trail, so steep it's as if she's above me, and I give my body one final push.

This time, it hurts. My lungs are burning, my legs so numb I can hardly feel them, hardly realize they're moving.

I think of Stacey. Of how proud she'd be if she could see me win. I reach up and touch her hat. *Running for Stacey*, as Roman said to me before the race.

Wait. Why did Roman say that? I never mentioned that to anyone. Not even David.

Roman said it when he saw the hat. Stacey's hat. He must've recognized it from back when she used to wear it.

Except that it was new. She'd worn it for the first time that day. The day she died.

And Roman had seen it.

The truth hits me like one of those gigantic boulders, nearly bringing me to my knees.

It was Roman.

I feel my legs going out from under me, and I'm on the ground, knees frozen in the snow.

No. Get up.

I touch Stacey's hat and leap to my feet. I see Erica up ahead, but now it's not her I'm looking for. I'm looking for Roman. He must have finished by now.

When I run up alongside Erica, I hear her breathing intensify, her little gasp of surprise. I feel her increase her stride, and we run side by side, the finish line in sight ahead of us, the sounds of people cheering from the sidelines.

But then I see Roman, so tall he stands heads above almost everyone, and I see the look of surprise on his face as he sees me racing for the finish. I am so focused on him that I barely notice leaving Erica behind.

And as I meet Roman's gaze, I wonder if he sees the fury in my eyes and in my runner's pace. It's only from the corner of my eye that I see a yellow ribbon being raised, and it's only in the distance that I hear cheers and cow bells, and all of a sudden Roman's face disappears, and he's gone.

And then I feel the ribbon on my chest, wrapping around my arms, the gentle touch of nylon that says you've won.

# Twenty-four

From the top, Mount Lithia feels like an island, floating in a sea of clouds.

I feel as though I'm on the highest peak of the island, as I stand on a makeshift podium, overlooking the other two hundred runners along with their families and friends. The winner's podium.

Somehow I did it—I won the women's race. I still don't know how. Maybe I was helped along by the spirits Alex believes in. Maybe my emotions are a stronger fuel than I ever knew.

Or maybe I am just good at running.

I should be happy, grateful. I know I should muster a smile for the crowds. But I've done this for Stacey, and when I think about her, all I can think about is the person standing next to me. The winner of the men's race.

Roman.

It is a Cloudline tradition for the winners to present the first-place medals to each other. And I don't know how I will be able to look at Roman now that I know what I know.

It all makes sense now. The secrets he kept alluding to. The haunted look in his eyes. I know that, deep down, he feels guilty about the wrongs he has committed, but my sympathy is spent. I think of how he kept trying to put me in the same category he is in—as if our secrets are the same. But they are not. Even through the haze of my own guilt I can see that our crimes are different.

Roman is holding my medal in his hand, dangling from a shimmering blue ribbon. He turns toward me, and I avoid making eye contact as I lean my head forward so that he can slip it around my neck. As he does, he whispers in my ear.

"Congratulations, Katherine. I knew you could do it."

I say nothing. Someone hands me Roman's medal, and it's my turn to reciprocate. I hear applause, and I turn back to Roman, still trying to avoid looking at him. I can't bear to see his face.

He lowers his head, and I place the medal around his neck. And I whisper into his ear.

"I know it was you."

He pulls his head back, and finally I meet his eyes. He is still smiling, basking in the attention. So I try again.

"Stacey," I say. "I know it was you who killed her."

His face swivels toward mine, revealing a flash of shock. Then the actor in him takes over, and his face goes blank. "I'm sorry."

"No, you're not," I say. "But you will be."

I turn away and step down from the podium. I push my way through the crowd and begin walking back down the hill. I hear someone shouting my name through the sounds of the crowd, but I keep walking.

When I feel a hand on my shoulder, I whirl around, expecting Roman. But it's David.

"What's your hurry?" he says, smiling. "Don't you want to stick around and enjoy the moment?"

"I—I'm just exhausted, that's all."

David is beaming, the happiest I've seen him since I first arrived in town. He reaches over and examines the medal hanging from around my neck.

"Stacey would be proud," he says. "You did great."

I lean into him, tears mixing with perspiration.

"It's okay," he says, and I lose track of time again, of how long I cry on his shoulder. This time it's not the forest but David taking care of me—and I'm grateful for him, for all, human and otherwise, who have sheltered me since I've arrived in Lithia. Whether I'm deserving of their care or not.

David offers me a ride back to town, but I tell him I need

to walk it off. It's true that I'm exhausted, but it's not what he thinks—it's a mental weariness, one that can only be overcome by driving the body to the point of collapse.

It's a long, long walk down, back through the cloud. But at this point the lack of visibility suits me just fine. Because I don't know what I'll do when I get to the bottom of this mountain.

I walk down the trail, passing volunteers who are cleaning up discarded water cups, taking down trail markers. By the time I get down to the road, the traffic cones are gone, the streets open again.

A car pulls over ahead of me. An old beat-up Subaru covered with bumper stickers. Alex.

He steps out of the car, watching me. "We have to stop meeting this way," he says.

"Don't worry," I say. "I'm not leaving town this time."

"Good," he says. "Does that mean I can give you a ride?"

Suddenly my legs feel as worn out as my brain, and they begin to shake. "I would like that."

He seems to sense how unsteady I am; he comes over, puts his arm around my waist, and begins leading me to the car. I notice that he, too, is still wearing his running clothes, and suddenly realize that I hadn't seen him at the finish. I'd been so upset about Stacey, so obsessed with Roman. "How'd you do?" I ask. "In the race?"

He grins. "I let Roman win. Again."

"Clearly. I wish you hadn't."

He shrugs. "I don't run to win," he says. "Never have."

"Why didn't I see you at the finish?"

We reach the car, and he opens the door for me. "Because I was behind you."

"What?" I'm confused. Alex had started running with me, then pulled ahead. I'd assumed he'd finished way up with the elite male runners. "How—"

"Shhh," he says, and puts a warm hand against my cold, tired face. "I sensed something happening to you out there. I just wanted to make sure you were all right."

"But—" I think of that ghostly form that had sent me back into the race, right back to where I needed to be. "But I didn't see you. I didn't see you anywhere."

"Doesn't mean I wasn't there," he says.

I wrap my arms around Alex's neck. I see now that I don't need to see everything, that sometimes the most important things are, like the mountain shrouded in clouds, hidden from ordinary view.

And then he kisses me, and I forget all about my tired legs and weary mind. I forget everything but Alex and me, together, the medal I've won pressed between our bodies as we stand by the side of the road.

—∿∿—

When we get back to town, I ask Alex to drop me off at the cemetery. He offers to stay, but I tell him I need to be alone. That I will see him later. He promises to take me out to dinner, to celebrate.

On my way to my mother's grave, I pass the headstone marked ROMAN, and I wonder how many others he has taken from their loved ones, and how long he has been at it. Hundreds of years? Thousands?

I arrive at my mother's grave and feel the ground slipping beneath me. I fall to my knees and begin to talk to her. I hope she is listening, somewhere, as I tell her all about the race. About Stacey. About Roman and Alex and how little I know about men. About how much I wish she were here to guide me.

And I also tell her that I feel she *is* guiding me, somehow—that as alone as I have felt over the years, she must be with me in some way because I have landed on my feet. I've made it back to Lithia, and I've finally chosen the right man, and I'm starting my life over again. It's still too hard to believe I've done it all on my own.

I reach out and touch her headstone, running my hands along the letters that make up her name. The name that we share—Healy—my name, which I've hidden for too long.

Maybe this investigator showing up was a good thing. Maybe it's time that I stop hiding. Time to be who I am, who I really am. To start over, here in Lithia where it all began. This time, I can dare to hope for a happier ending.

Hearing footsteps, I wipe the tears from my eyes and stand up. When I look over to see who it is, I feel fury rise within my tired body. It's Roman.

I know that I could find it within me to run—anger being the strongest fuel of all—but I am finished running. Especially from him.

So I stand as tall as I can. "How dare you come here," I say. "I don't want you anywhere near me."

"I came to apologize."

"There is nothing you can say to make me forgive you."

"Please," he says. "Give me a chance."

"For what?"

"Let me try to change," he says. "I know I can be that person you want me to be."

"I don't believe you can, Roman. I thought at first that you could, that I could help. But you're beyond help."

"Katherine, there will be no more secrets between us anymore. I promise."

I'm staring at him, and that's when I realize that he's looking at my mother's grave. My heart skips as I make the connection.

"Oh, no," I say. "You didn't—"

He cuts me off. "No."

"You killed her, too," I say, "didn't you?"

"No," he repeats. "I—"

"First my mother, then Stacey. Who else are you going to take from me, Roman?"

"Katherine—"

"Don't keep telling me you can change," I say. "You've been here forever, preying on humans. That's why I looked familiar to you when you first met me, isn't it?"

"Yes," he says. "Yes, I knew your mother—but I did not hurt your mother."

"Why should I believe you?"

"I swear. I swear on my grave, or what used to be my grave."

"That means nothing."

"She didn't die of a bear attack," he says. "That much is true."

"Then what happened?"

But he is already turning, walking away. I shout after him, "What happened, Roman?"

He doesn't answer. And it doesn't matter. She is gone. Just like Stacey. And nothing will bring her back.

There is still one more thing I came here to do.

I remember that at my mother's burial, my grandmother

had given me a shiny blue pebble to place on her headstone. She told me that flowers die, but a stone—a piece of the earth—will last forever.

My grandmother is gone now, too, and I am not sure whether she knew that I never put that little pebble on my mother's headstone. I had taken it eagerly, but I had been so distracted that day that I must've forgotten—I discovered it in my pocket a week later, in the car as my dad drove us to Houston. By then it was a different memory, a memory of everything else that would soon disappear.

But I held onto that stone, and now, I pull it out of the little inner pocket of my running shorts, where I'd put it for luck. I place it on her headstone. From now on, it belongs here. From now on, I will make my own luck.

Then I make my way to Stacey's grave. The ground is still soft; the sod laid down above her has not yet taken root. I take the medal from around my neck, and I lay it across Stacey's headstone.

The sky is clearing as I slowly walk back into town. Back to my little cottage. To David and my job. To Alex. And into a future of unknowns.